DEADLY TRUTH

The private detective pushed himself away from the window and wondered if he were dreaming or had just witnessed a ritual murder. He wished he could take a picture because there was no way in hell that anyone would believe this story. He stuck his eye back at the hole. The man lifted a cylinder onto his shoulder. A dozen more cylinders leaned against the back wall. Each contained a woman in a silver bodysuit.

The detective fought his way out of the shrubs and started up the dark roadway. The hell with Borley, he had to call the cops. He would go to the cops right now, tell them what he saw, and make them swear out a search warrant.

He heard the tires screech just before the headlights came on. He never had a chance. The woman's face on the other side of the windshield grinned and his last thought was that the car was his own.

■ ■ ■

THE
PERSEUS
BREED

KEVIN EGAN

PAGEANT BOOKS

PAGEANT BOOKS
225 Park Avenue South
New York, New York 10003

Cover artwork by David Mattingly

Printed in the U.S.A.

First Pageant Books printing: December, 1988

10 9 8 7 6 5 4 3 2 1

For my parents and for Mary Lou

Special thanks to Marcia Rich

Our birth is but a sleep and a forgetting:
The Soul that rises with us, our life's Star,
    Hath had elsewhere its setting,
      And cometh from afar:
    Not in entire forgetfulness
    And not in utter nakedness,
But trailing clouds of glory do we come

        —William Wordsworth
          Ode
          Intimations of Immortality

THE **PERSEUS BREED**

Prologue

———◆———

THE BUS KICKED gravel onto his pants and into the weeds as it pulled away. He stood for a long moment and listened as the whine of the engine died among the trees. The dirt road ran straight between a cornfield and an empty pasture, then curved into the pines. He could reach the farmhouse while there was still light in the sky. They could sit on the front porch swing, as they had in July, and watch the fields turn blue. But something stopped him. He toed a large stone from the clay of the road and examined it for fossils. It was smooth. He heaved the stone into the pasture, then picked up another and another until he found one pitted by tiny seashells. He put the stone with its ancient imprints into his sack, then started up the road.

Lights burned in the farmhouse, giving it a

jack-o'-lantern look against the blue hills. His pace quickened on the rutted path that crossed the patch of weeds she called her lawn. The screen door squeaked open and clapped shut behind him. He called her name.

She was not in the kitchen. Rice and green beans simmered on the stove. Chicken crackled in the oven. Batter sat thickly in a biscuit tin. He went out the back door. The rocky garden she tilled for salad stuff was deserted. Tomato plants drooped away from their stakes.

She had to be upstairs. He took two beers from the refrigerator and eased open the door to the room she used as a studio. The bird prints, usually scattered around the room like so many feathers, were neatly piled. The surreal canvas he had titled *American Gothic 2100 A.D.* was uncovered on its easel.

He ran down to the living room. The dolls were still on the bookcase. Three sat just as he had left them, their eyes open, their arms reaching up for Mama. But the one she had christened Baby Valerie lay on its side, its eyes staring up at him.

He plopped onto the front porch swing, the beer bottles sweating in his hands. By the time he finished one, it was dark. By the time he finished the other, he knew she was not coming back.

Chapter One

———◆———

ON THE MORNING that Professor Borley Share left Ithaca, an egg truck overturned on Route 13 and snarled traffic for two miles. Borley sat behind a Winnebago and watched the temperature gauge of his idling Starion edge up to the red zone. He was heating up himself. The old woman had sounded unreceptive on the telephone. Even when he said he was the scientist investigating her daughter's disappearance, she barely responded. If he arrived late, she might refuse to see him.

The Winnebago sputtered forward in a cloud of oil smoke, allowing Borley to roll past the damaged egg truck, which was tethered to a crane, and men in overalls who slopped yolk and shells into a storm sewer. The traffic soon thinned. Automobile dealerships and fast-food restaurants dissolved into a valley of rugged farmland. Borley shot around the Winnebago, keeping his foot on the pedal and a tight rein on the wheel as the highway spilled along the valley floor in long sweeping curves.

He passed under a railway trestle, then turned onto a clay and crushed-shale road that ran straight between a cornfield and a pine forest toward a rise in the middle of the valley floor. Beyond the rise, Borley could see white flickering in the dark of the trees. The white resolved into the walls of summer cottages, then the trees separated to reveal station wagons, barbecue pits, and a lake with boats. Something flew in front of the Starion and Borley hit the brakes. A red Frisbee skittered into the ditch along the side of the road. He heard children giggling. Then a girl showed her face in the weeds.

"Sorry, mister."

Borley tapped his horn and drove on. The tar-paper house was beyond the cottages on a bleak rise that it shared with a dead thorn tree. Borley pulled the Starion hard against the ditch and cut the engine. Insects buzzed and Queen Anne's lace bobbed gently in the fields. The house had no porch. Three steps made of wood slats laid across cinder blocks led to a screen door sagging on its hinges. Borley, with his tape recorder hanging from his shoulder, cupped his hand over his eyes so he could peer inside. The old woman was seated in a rocking chair with her back to the door. Her left arm rested on a flimsy table.

"Come in and state your business," she said.

Borley opened the door and entered. The old

woman had thin arms and bony white ankles that poked out of her plaid dress and disappeared into two large slippers. Her midsection was heaped onto the seat of the chair as if all the flesh and muscle of her extremities had been sucked in and turned to jelly. She had a fly swatter in one hand and, showing great economy of movement, dispatched three flies in as many attempts.

"It's good of you to see me like this, Mrs. Grover," he said.

The old woman nodded. She had a profile that belonged on a coin.

"What's that?" she said.

"A tape recorder," replied Borley as he unraveled the microphone cord. "It's easier than me taking notes. I'll just record everything you say."

Mrs. Grover flicked the swatter and knocked a fly out of the air. It lay on its back and beat its wings on the table until she mashed it.

"Damn new occasion that anyone wants to remember anything I say," she said.

Borley tested the tape recorder. There were shouts from outside as the Frisbee game moved closer.

"Funny, no matter where you go kids like to play in the street," he said.

"Summer people," said the old woman. "This used to be a nice place before they came. They don't care about anything because they don't really live here."

Borley finished adjusting the tape recorder and pulled up a chair.

"Now, Mrs. Grover," he said, "you understand that I'm here to talk about your daughter."

"My Sarah."

"The newspaper account I found last night said that she disappeared thirty years ago tomorrow. Is that correct?"

"If it's in the newspaper, it's right," said Mrs. Grover.

"The newspaper also said that you were recently widowed at the time and that you didn't report Sarah as missing for over a week," said Borley. The old woman stared at him. "I'm not interested in what the newspaper said. I want to know if there was anything strange about the disappearance that the article didn't mention."

"Isn't it strange when a daughter leaves her mother and the only home she ever knew, and ain't heard from again?"

"Of course," said Borley. "What I mean is, did Sarah act strange just before she disappeared? Did she act like a child? Play with dolls, perhaps."

"She didn't act like a child, exactly."

"What do you mean by exactly?"

"When Sarah was very young, my husband, that's Mr. Grover, hung a tire from a tree." Mrs. Grover nodded out the back door. In the distance, a dark stand of trees huddled in the bright field. "Sarah used to spend hours out on that tire, just swinging. Then one day, she started talking about a woman who came to see her when she was on the tire. I asked her who the woman was and she said just a nice big lady with thick black hair. Didn't sound like anyone I knowed, so I didn't think nothing of it. Didn't believe her, neither."

"Why not?"

"Mister, in those days I knew everybody in this valley. Besides, there was just one way in and one way out." She nodded at the road. "If anybody was in those trees with my Sarah, I would of knowed it. So I figured Sarah had one of those—"

"Imaginary friends?" said Borley.

"Right," said Mrs. Grover. "It was lonely being a little girl in this valley back then. Ain't so great being an old woman, either."

"How old was your daughter when this imaginary woman appeared?"

"'Bout eight, I guess." Mrs. Grover stared out at the trees.

"I'm sorry," said Borley. "You were saying."

Mrs. Grover focused on the tape recorder.

"When Sarah was in high school, she met a fella from up Ithaca way named Donnelly. He was crazy about her and she was crazy about him. He wanted to marry her and take her away to California. I wasn't big on California, but I knew that anyplace was better than this valley. Then one day, Sarah just turned her back on him. Didn't want nothing to do with him no more. He came to me, but there was nothing I could do. Sarah knew her own mind, always did."

"This is all very interesting, Mrs. Grover."

"Hold your tongue. You asked about my Sarah acting like a child. Well, I'm going to tell you. I never asked Sarah about young Donnelly, and she never told me nothing. That was okay. Sarah always knew her own mind. But long after, late one night, she came to me with a funny look in her eye, like someone done that thing to her with the pocket watch."

"Hypnotized her."

"Yeah. She told me the reason she broke off with young Donnelly was because the woman in the trees told her to. A day later, she went off."

Mrs. Grover turned back to the distant stand of trees.

"I was sad but never really surprised that she left."

"Not surprised?" said Borley.

"It was like someone gave her to me for a while and then took her away again," said Mrs. Grover.

"Wasn't she yours?"

"Oh, she was mine, all right. I mean I bore her and raised her. I just don't know who else she belonged to."

"But your husband—"

Mrs. Grover shook her head. A fly landed on the table within the reach of her swatter, but the old woman's eyes looked past it. The few teeth she had left gnawed at the inside of her cheek.

"When I was a girl," she said, "in the days when you could live here and not have people come from far away and ruin things, my family had a farm. It was during the summer, August, I think. We had thunderstorms all day, hailstones as big as your fist, and there was talk of tornadoes. The door to the hayloft of the barn used to blow open in storms, and I went out to make sure it was closed so the hay didn't get wet. The wind tore a plank off just as I was going into the barn. Hit me right in the head.

"They told me I was out for about two hours. My daddy found me about an hour after I got hit and I didn't come around until about an hour after that. By then the doc was there. They took me to the hospital up in Ithaca for a few days. I spent a lot of time sleeping with those pills they gave me. About a month later I learned I was with child."

Mrs. Grover paused to let the words sink in.

"So you are telling me that you conceived Sarah while you were in the hospital," said Borley.

"No. I'm telling you I was a virgin, but I was with child."

"You must be mistaken."

"Mister, I was a virgin when that plank came down and whupped me in the head. And I was a virgin when I left that hospital. But I was with child sure as I'm sitting here."

"These things have happened," said Borley.

"I ain't never heard of it," said Mrs. Grover. " 'Cept once."

"It isn't uncommon, and there are logical explanations."

"Name one."

"Did you do any swimming in a public pool before the accident?"

"We didn't have one around here then. Still don't, that I know of, unless these newcomers are building one, which wouldn't surprise me none."

"What about any other body of water used by a lot of people?"

"The only swimming I did was in that lake

these newcomers use," Mrs. Grover said testily. "It wasn't ever crowded, except with bullfrogs."

"This sounds crude," said Borley, "but you might have been raped while you were unconscious in the hospital."

"Doubt it. Too many nurses around all the time," said Mrs. Grover. "Besides, I shared a room with a young girl like me. I forget what she was there for, but the heat used to bother her. I had the bed closest to the window, but on a few hot nights we switched so that she could sleep better. 'Course, that was against the rules, but we didn't care."

"All right, I believe you," said Borley.

Mrs. Grover smirked, unconvinced.

"Did your daughter know what you thought about her birth?"

"Of course not."

"Did she ever ask you whether she was adopted?"

"Once she said something about her real parents being a king and a queen. I figured she was reading some of those fairy tales, and told her so. She never said nothing again."

"How old was she then?"

"Young."

"About the same age as when her imaginary friend appeared?"

"Maybe," said Mrs. Grover.

"How did Sarah disappear?" said Borley.

"It was the day after she told me why she broke off with young Donnelly," said Mrs. Grover. "I woke up to the sound of her banging around the kitchen. It was early. I came out and saw her dressed like it was Sunday. She was cooking a big breakfast, but she had only one place set on the table, for me.

"She didn't say nothing while I ate, even though I tried to get her to talking. She went outside, and while I washed the dishes I noticed her walking out toward them trees. She was stumbling, I figured because she was wearing her good shoes, and walking ain't easy in these fields.

"She never came back. Around dusk, I went out to look. Her shoes were on the ground, and the tire was swinging like the wind blowed it."

"Did you see anyone or anything?"

"No," said Mrs. Grover. "I thought I heard something like a car motor. But when I got back to the field, whatever it was was gone."

There was a long silence. A pained look came over the old woman's face.

"Sir, did you come here to help me find my daughter?"

"No. I'm afraid that's not why I'm here."

"Then I don't want to talk anymore."

Borley silently rolled up the microphone cord, gathered his equipment, and headed for the door. The old woman's voice stopped him.

"I wish she had gone to California," she said without turning around. "Anything's better than this."

Borley went down the crude steps. The air outside was warmer now, the buzzing of the insects louder. He took the dirt road back to the highway.

The Frisbee game was over. The cottages were bright in the sun. When he reached the highway, he set the cruise control at seventy, switched on his radar detector, and pointed the Starion homeward.

Chapter Two

—◆—

THE CAMPUS OF the State College at Purchase was quiet. The Humanities Building was completely empty. Borley let himself in through a side entrance. Fluorescent lights hummed in the corridors, and the air smelled faintly of fresh paint. His office was an inferno. He wedged open the door with a chair and closed the blinds against the late afternoon sun. The red light of his telephone answering machine was blinking, urgently, he thought, but it could have been his frame of mind. Before he could replay the messages, the telephone rang. He let the machine answer and turned up the volume in order to hear the incoming message.

"My name is Bill Shaw and I'm calling about your ad for the psychological study. I am an adult and I did have a recent recurrence of a childhood adoption fantasy. I had it about a month ago. I would like to take part in the study. I can be reached at 732–4746. Thank you."

The machine clicked off. The counter showed fifteen calls. Borley reversed the tape and listened to the messages. The first was from a student who wanted to discuss his final grade. The next twelve were responses to the classified ad. Nine of these callers were men. Borley ignored them. Two of the three women sounded hesitant and did not leave phone numbers. The third was a Patricia Brady. Borley wrote her name and number on a pad. The fourteenth caller was Karen, who guessed that he might stop at the office on his way home and suggested that he pick up a steak for dinner. Then came Bill Shaw's call.

Borley erased the tape and dialed Patricia Brady's phone number. He introduced himself as the professor who was conducting the psychological study.

"Oh, I'm so happy you called," said Patricia Brady. "I think psychology is just marvelous."

Borley agreed, but his interest sank. He was not looking for women who thought psychology was marvelous.

"The first thing I need is demographic information," he said. "How old are you?"

"Oh, if you're not the curious one," said Patricia Brady. "Forty-five."

"I see," said Borley. He asked several other questions—place of birth, occupation, education, marital status—and politely listened to the answers.

"When does it start?" said Patricia Brady. "I hope not for another week. I'm very busy right now."

"It won't be for at least a week. I will contact you."

Borley cut short her enthusiastic good-bye. He unlocked the top drawer of his desk and placed the tape of the Grover interview in with the others. These interviews merely confirmed what he already knew. His classified ad had been running for over two months in psychology journals, self-help magazines, and the personal sections of local newspapers. He had been receiving an average of ten calls per day, mostly from college students and middle-aged housewives. None were right. In order to find the answer, he needed at least one response from a twenty-nine-year-old woman with an unresolved adoption fantasy. In another month, it would be too late.

He locked the drawer and headed home.

Borley owned a house at the end of a cul-de-sac just outside the town of Katonah. He pulled in behind Karen's car on the shady side of the driveway and let the Starion idle down. He carried the steak and two bottles of red wine he had bought on impulse. Once inside he sensed Karen was in the small ground-floor bedroom she had fashioned into a study. Karen was writing another novel. Ever since Borley met her she had been writing a novel, though never the same one for very long. She had a knack for thinking up entertaining plots and writing pithy character sketches, but once the groundwork was done she lost interest. When Borley was feeling critical, her inability to complete a project bothered him.

He peeked into the study. Computer paper cascaded from a file cabinet, rippled across the floor, and mounted the table near Karen's shoulder. Her arms were folded under her head. The word processor monitor showed a full screen of text. The forgotten cursor blinked slowly.

Borley leaned down and brushed a kiss on her cheek. He noticed a gray hair springing from behind her ear. Karen, the eternal student, was aging, too. She slowly sat up.

"I hope your readers will stay awake," said Borley.

"Very funny," Karen said after a yawn. She studied the screen then turned off the word processor. "How was the seminar?"

"The usual bullshit."

"If all these seminars are the usual bullshit, why do you keep going?"

"It is important to make an appearance," said Borley. "Besides, they only seem like bullshit in retrospect."

"I see," said Karen.

She hugged him. Borley was much taller than she. He used to say their bodies fit well together anyway, but today her nose poking beneath his sternum made him squirm.

"Did you pick up the steak?" she said.

"And some wine." He looked across the room at notes Karen had taped to the wall. He wondered what story she was writing this time. He never asked anymore, and she had stopped telling him.

* * *

After dinner, Karen suggested they drive to a secluded field to watch the annual Perseid meteor shower. They brought a blanket, a bottle of wine, and two glasses.

"Why did we wait until midnight?" said Borley. The ground under the blanket was comfortably rutted. The wine spread warmth. Karen lifted her head from his lap.

"Because that is when the earth is turned in the direction of the meteors."

She pointed them out, pinpricks of light in the dim constellation known as Perseus. Borley counted five in less than a minute.

"Why are they so small?"

"You sound like a child," laughed Karen. "They are debris left by a comet. Most are smaller than pebbles."

"I'm not very good outside my discipline," said Borley.

"And I know a little of everything," said Karen. "But I happen to love the sky."

"Have you ever seen anything out of the ordinary?"

"Wow!" she said, sitting up. Borley followed her gaze and caught a flurry of meteors dying in the purple sky. "You mean that isn't enough?"

"We know what they are. I'm talking about something unexplained."

Karen lowered her head onto his lap. She balanced her wineglass on her stomach.

"Twice," she said. "The first time I was in college, before I met you. I was in a field with my boyfriend one night. A huge light with a bluish dome rose slowly from behind the trees at the far end of the field. It was a quarter mile away at most. We stared at it until we both sensed that it was watching us, too. Then we ran like hell.

"The second time, I was with a group of people on a beach. Someone noticed that a bunch of stars at the top of the sky were moving, not in any one direction, but back and forth as if they were having a meeting. We watched them for an hour."

"Did you report them?" said Borley.

"My boyfriend and I were out in that field smoking dope. I never hallucinate, but the fact remains we were smoking. The beach party was on the Fourth of July."

"No wonder you never mention them," said Borley.

"Just my luck to see UFOs like that," said Karen. "It's as if they knew there would be a more logical explanation."

"I know what you mean," said Borley.

Karen sat up and swung her legs around until she faced him. Her features were visible even in the dark. They sharpened whenever she became angry.

"Did you really attend a seminar at Oneonta?" she said.

"Yes," said Borley.

There was a tense silence. Neither looked up at the meteors.

"All right," he continued. "I went to Ithaca, too."

"The farmhouse, right?"

"Karen, I've told you before. The farmhouse

was torn down years ago for a mobile-home park."

"Then why did you go there?"

"I arranged with an editor of the *Ithaca Journal* to look through the new microfilm archives. I found an article I had missed about the disappearance of a woman named Sarah Grover. Her mother still lives in a shack in a valley south of Ithaca. She agreed to talk to me. She claims her daughter resulted from a parthenogenetic birth, but otherwise it is a classic case. They lived in isolated circumstances and the daughter was approximately thirty when she experienced a recurrence of her childhood adoption fantasy. Then she disappeared without any hint of foul play. There even was mention of the woman with the long dark hair."

"The woman is probably a serial killer."

"Don't you see, the woman isn't real," said Borley. "She's a manifestation of the syndrome."

"I thought you satisfied this obsession last summer," said Karen.

"I resent you calling it an obsession."

"What else should I call it when someone is completely wrapped up in the past, nostalgia?"

"I admit it started as a personal quest, but now it's pure scientific inquiry. And I didn't satisfy either the obsession or the inquiry last summer. How could I? This is the summer that all the data points to."

"I don't want to hear it," said Karen.

"Fine. But I will prove the syndrome exists, and I will prove it this summer."

Karen jumped up and strode away. Borley

looked at the sky. It was only the beginning of August and already these arguments were becoming too frequent.

He gathered the wine bottle and glasses into the blanket and slung it over his shoulder. The Starion was parked under an oddly shaped tree just visible against the sky. Suddenly, the dark grass turned pale green. Karen appeared sitting on the Starion's hood, and a light that looked like a white sun bounced off the windshield into his eyes. He turned. A huge fireball fell toward him, throwing off sparks and obliterating the stars. Borley dove to the ground. The air above him hissed. He expected an explosion, but the grass darkened and the hissing vanished. He rolled over. A bright circle of light slipped quickly below the horizon, and the stars returned to the sky.

"What the hell was that!"

Karen did not answer. Borley hastily repacked his blanket and stumbled toward the car.

"I thought they all were pebbles," he said.

Karen jumped off the hood. "Must have been a larger piece of debris," she said flatly.

Borley looked up at the luminous trail crossing the sky.

"Maybe it was something else."

"Borley, this was a meteor shower, so that was a meteor. Just like on the Fourth of July, when every UFO is a firecracker."

They were silent as they drove home along the looping roads. Karen quickly went inside. Borley leaned against the Starion and tilted his head until he saw nothing but sky. The fireball's trail, lit by a waning moon, slowly separated. He wondered about the earliest astronomers, men who stood on lonely hilltops and saw the fiery demise of a cosmic pebble as a message from the gods. He was standing on a hilltop himself, convinced that a psychological syndrome with a physiological trigger was causing women to disappear with clockwork regularity. But the implication of Karen's last statement weighed heavily. No matter what he called his investigation, it still was his obsession.

Borley found Karen typing madly in her study. He felt her sense his presence in the doorway, but she did not turn around. He went upstairs to bed. They usually discussed their differences intelligently, but each turned inward when the disappearances came up. Karen was embarrassed by her irrational jealousy over someone Borley had not seen in thirty years. Borley was more than confused by the intensity of her feelings, but he also realized she was a perceptive woman; she might understand him better than he cared to admit.

Borley was still awake when Karen entered the room. He lay motionless and watched her remove her clothes. She went into the bathroom for a shower and returned without having dried herself. Her body glistened in the weak moonlight, and her long dark hair formed two slick lines over her small breasts. She settled next to him without disturbing the bed. He touched her shoulder and another bout of silence ended.

After Karen's breathing evened into sleep, Borley slipped out of bed and went downstairs to the back door. He walked across the wet grass to a dilapidated toolshed and paused with his hand on the doorknob. The only sound was the rush of trucks on the distant interstate. There was no sign of Karen at the bedroom window. He unlocked the door and reached for the flashlight he kept on the floor inside.

He played the light around a room with bright yellow plasterboard walls and a polished wood floor. A fake dresser, which concealed two file cabinets, stood against the rear wall next to a molding that represented a conceptual window. A small daybed occupied the far left corner. Above the bed was a huge wall-map of New York State. On the floor along the right wall were two neat stacks of framed prints. Each print was a realistic depiction of a bird.

Borley directed the light to a painting on an easel in the middle of the room. Silver towers stood against a purple sky powdered with stars and sliced by three crescent moons. A parade of stylized people, paired off in couples, followed a winding road into an austere building. The parade continued out the other side of the building and weaved toward the right foreground. It ended with two large faceless people, one male the other female, standing side by side.

As Borley stared at the couple for whom he had titled the painting *American Gothic 2100 A.D.*, the UFO discussion came to mind.

"Just my luck to have fallen in love with a crazy woman," he muttered.

Chapter Three

———◆———

TWO DAYS AFTER the night in the field, Borley received a phone call from a woman named Kate Lyons. She explained she had noticed the classified ad while looking for job opportunities in the local newspaper. Recently she had experienced a recurrence of a childhood adoption fantasy. She was twenty-nine years old. Borley arranged to meet her at eleven o'clock that same morning.

Ten minutes later, the telephone rang again. A woman named Gina Lo Biasi told a story similar to Kate's. The only difference was that she had noticed the ad in a self-help magazine while searching for a therapist. Borley asked her to come in at one o'clock that afternoon.

Kate Lyons did not arrive at eleven, or even at twelve. Borley paced behind his desk and rushed to the door whenever a sound echoed in the quiet building. Finally, he heard the regular tap of heels approaching along the corridor's marble floor. He sat at his desk and pretended to be busy. The tapping slowed, then stopped. When he looked up, Kate Lyons was standing in the doorway. She had bright blond hair and a deep tan set off by a white dress cinched at the waist with a red belt. She hesitated.

"I know," said Borley. "You expected a horde of white rats running in a maze and test tubes filled with boiling liquids."

Kate forced a smile. She accepted Borley's invitation to sit and arranged herself carefully on a chair facing the desk. Borley noticed a brown thigh curving through the slit in her dress.

"Am I dressed okay?" said Kate. "I didn't know what to wear to an experiment, so I picked white."

"You look fine," said Borley. "But it's not an experiment, it's a study."

"I get paid though, don't I?"

"A small fee, as the ad said."

"Then technically I have a job."

"Technically, I guess you do," said Borley. "Though I wouldn't want to depend on it."

"At least I can tell Marty I did something."

Borley noticed her wedding band. "Is Marty your husband?"

"Yeah. He's a real sweetheart, but lately he's been in a bad mood. His job's not going so great and we're tight for money, so he wants me to work."

"Sounds reasonable," said Borley.

"He wants me to become a secretary. How does he expect me to type?" Kate held up her hands. Her fingernails were long and they exactly matched the red of her belt. "So I've been looking through the want ads but for my kind of job. Acting or modeling."

"I see," said Borley. "Let me explain what I'm looking for. Most people have an adoption fantasy at some point in their childhood. A few have it to an intense degree, and fewer still have it unresolved as adults. But it does happen. I want to establish a profile of the type of people who have the recurring fantasy. Do you mind if I tape this?"

"Not at all," said Kate. She cleared her throat vigorously. "I've been taped before."

Borley realized he was expected to ask about her previous taping session, but he resisted. He placed the recorder on his desk then wrote her name, address, phone number, and date of birth on the label of a blank cassette. He started the machine.

"I don't think my parents wanted to have me," said Kate.

"How do you know that?"

"I always knew it, and my sisters knew it, too. They're twins, three years older than me. They had beautiful blond hair, but their features were pinched together at the ends of their faces. Marty always said they looked like they were weaned on lemons.

"They hated me because I was beautiful and they weren't. Whenever something broke in the house, they would blame me. My mother believed anything they said. I spent a lot of time alone in my room. I read fairy tales and began to refer to the twins as my stepsisters. I thought *step* meant *evil*."

"Is that where your fantasy came from?" said Borley.

"No, I always had the feeling. The twins were ugly, I was beautiful. They had blond hair, I had black. That's right. This isn't natural, but no one can tell. Not even professionals." Kate pulled a lock in front of her eyes and smirked. "The twins called it coal black. They told me that our parents didn't plan to have me. They said that my mother thought I was a tumor until she went to a doctor."

"Did you ever discuss this with your mother?" said Borley.

"My mother isn't the type of person who discusses things like that," said Kate. "But I did some snooping. She used to write down her thoughts in a notebook, like a diary. One day I sneaked up into the attic and read the book from the year I was born. The twins were right. My parents were using contraceptives, but there I was anyway."

"Then what you have told me is the truth, not fantasy," said Borley.

"My mother wasn't always honest with herself. I think she wrote what she wanted to be true. I believe she was pregnant and then lost the baby. It might have been accidental, it might have been on purpose. Anyway, she felt guilty and adopted me."

"Ever find any adoption records?"

"I looked, but I never found any. Then I decided I didn't need any more proof."

"More proof?" said Borley. "You haven't mentioned that you had any proof at all."

Kate tapped her temple with a long, elegant finger. "Up here I did. I knew I didn't belong to them. That was enough for me."

"Are your parents still alive?"

"My father died when I was in high school. He worked for the railroad and was killed in an accident. My mother sued, but the railroad lawyers said they could prove that the accident was his fault. We didn't get much money. I haven't spoken to my mother in years."

"And your sisters?"

Kate smirked. "I haven't seen them since the day I married Marty."

"You mentioned Marty before in connection with them. Were you all competing for him?"

"Marty was the high school dreamboat," she said wistfully. "He was class president, captain of the football team, and owned a car. He was in the twins' class, so he was three years older than me. He didn't pay attention to any of the high-school girls. He dated coeds from Oneonta State, which wasn't far from where we all lived. Then he noticed me. I was in eighth grade when we had our first date. We knew that night that we would be married."

"When did the fantasy resurface?" he said.

Kate lowered her eyes and focused on her hands knotted on her lap.

"I mentioned how Marty wants me to work," she said. "Well, he set up an interview for me a couple of days ago. It was for a secretarial job. I actually got as far as the door, but I couldn't walk in. I went to Bloomingdale's instead and bought this dress. It was on sale."

Kate stood and did a pirouette. Her dress billowed about her. Borley noticed that she had nice legs. She sat again and turned somber. Her little show was over.

"Marty got home before I did. There was no point in lying. We had a big fight. He cut up all our credit cards and threatened divorce if I didn't find a job and stop throwing away his hard-earned money. Then he went out to eat at Burger King. He does that when he's mad at me because he comes home smelling of pickles and onions.

"Later, after he was asleep, I went into the bathroom to try a new eyeliner. I work with cosmetics to relax. All of a sudden, I felt this tremendous blast of heat, like the ceiling fan was a sunlamp. I almost fainted. When the heat passed, I had this urge to go outside. I took a long walk and did a lot of thinking. I began to feel the way I did when I was a little girl at the mercy of the twins. I didn't care if Marty divorced me. I had my plan and I was going to stick to it. Then I saw this big light fly across the sky and I knew that I was right. The feeling hasn't left me since."

Borley switched off the tape recorder and leaned back in his chair.

"What do you think?" said Kate.

"I don't. I gather information."

"No, about me," said Kate. "Do you think I'll make it career-wise?"

"Actress or model?"

"Either, I'm not picky."

"People have a way of getting what they deserve," said Borley. He turned away from her beaming smile and reached for a metal box labeled PETTY CASH on the credenza. Inside were two twenties, a ten, and some loose change for the photocopy machine.

"Sorry it can't be more," he said as he pushed the ten across his desk.

"It will help," said Kate. "I'm going to Cape Cod next week. Marty doesn't know it. He'll be away on business himself. Did you know that the Cape is a good place to be discovered?"

"No, I didn't," said Borley.

"It's true. A lot of stars got their start there. Most people don't know, but I've read about it."

"Good luck," said Borley. "I will be in touch if I need to talk further."

Kate flashed a pinup smile. Borley ushered her out of the office. Another woman was in the corridor. She paced nervously, her hands clutching a purse, but she stopped the moment she noticed Borley and Kate.

"Gina Lo Biasi?" said Borley.

"I'm sorry, I'm early," said Gina.

"No problem," said Borley. "Have a seat inside. I will be with you in a minute."

He escorted Kate to the front door of the building and watched her walk to a blue Toyota with a badly dented door. He memorized the license-plate number as she drove away.

Chapter Four

———◆———

GINA LO BIASI was a tall, thin woman who gave no shape to a stiff pair of jeans. Her face was pale except for red worry-lines around her mouth and across her brow. Still, Borley thought she could be attractive if she took care of herself.

"That woman," said Gina. "Did she answer your ad, too?"

"Yes." Borley wrote a description of Kate's car and the license-plate number on her cassette.

"I'm surprised someone so beautiful could have problems."

"Participating in my study isn't necessarily the sign of a problem," said Borley. He noted her name, address, phone number, and date of birth on the label of a fresh cassette. He asked her to put her purse on the floor. The sight of her fingers clawing into the leather made him nervous.

"I come from an old-style Italian family," Gina said after Borley described the purpose of his study. "My father was a stone mason. My mother spent all her life in the kitchen or the laundry. Do you know what I mean?"

Borley nodded.

"I used to have this dream when I was a little girl. It was about my parents. You know how in a dream you are sure who the people are even if they don't look like them. Well, these people didn't look like my parents, but they were."

"Who did they look like?" said Borley.

"I can't remember their faces," said Gina. "They might not even have had any. But I do remember their clothes. They always wore something different—three piece suits, tennis outfits, fancy gowns. My real parents didn't own anything like that."

"What happened in these dreams?"

"Nothing," said Gina. "They would just stand side by side."

"What was so important about the dreams?" said Borley.

"The feeling," said Gina. "It was always so intense that I would walk around the next day believing that the dream was reality and that my waking life was the dream. It started again."

"When?"

"I have to give you some background. My husband and I haven't been getting along for the last year. Ralph's Italian, too, and having a big family means a lot to him. We tried to have a baby for years with no luck. Finally, last summer, my doctor told us I was sterile. Ralph exploded and I started to feel guilty."

Borley shifted in his chair. Kate Lyons wanted to be flattered and now Gina Lo Biasi wanted to discuss her crumbling marriage.

Gina noticed his impatience. "I'm getting to the point. About a month ago, things started disappearing from the house. They were little things—kitchen utensils, household tools, towels. At first, I thought that Ralph was trying to drive me crazy, the way Charles Boyer did to Ingrid Bergman in that movie. I didn't let it bother me because I knew what he was doing. Then, about a week ago, I found out that Ralph was setting up an apartment. It stopped me dead in my tracks."

"And that is when you started having the dream again?"

"No," said Gina. "That was when I started having trouble sleeping. I sat in the house with the lights off and waited in case he came to steal a couch or a table. The whole week was a blur, but I distinctly remember when the dream began again. It was two nights ago. I fell asleep in the living room and dreamed that I was floating down a river. The river looked like a stream that I used to play along as a girl, only it was much wider. It flowed past some fields, through a forest, then ended at a futuristic-type house. It was silver and had narrow windows and towers that looked like rockets. There was a little front porch that wasn't futuristic but looked more like something you'd see on a farm. My parents, at least the people I assumed were my parents, were standing on the porch. They were dressed all in white. I thought that they were a doctor and a nurse, but now I'm not sure what kind of clothes they were wearing."

"Did they do anything or say anything?"

"No," said Gina. "They just stood side by side on the porch, like the farm couple in that old painting."

Borley opened his desk drawer. In a file folder was a photograph he had taken of *American Gothic 2100 A.D.* The photo was enlarged, then cropped so that it was a four-by-seven print of the painting alone. He placed it face down on the desk.

"How did you feel when you woke up?" he said.

"The way I felt when I had the dream as a little girl. I went outside to a gazebo we have in the back yard. I leaned against it and stared up at the sky. The dream was more real to me than my own life. I stared for a long time, until that huge meteor flew over and snapped me out of it. I went back inside. The stove light was on. It hadn't been on before and my electric frying pan was gone. Ralph must have been there while I was outside. I didn't even hear him."

Gina stopped to take a deep breath. "I've had that dream every time I've fallen asleep since. I even have it when I doze off in the afternoon. I'm worried because I want that dream to be true. I shouldn't. I'm an adult. What should I do?"

"I'm sorry, but I'm a professor, not a practicing psychologist. The purpose of my study is to gather information, not provide counseling."

"Oh," said Gina. She lowered her eyes to her tense knuckles, then looked up. "What have you found out?"

"That a lot of people have similar feelings, though no two manifestations are exactly alike." Borley tapped the edge of the photograph on the desktop. "I don't know anything else."

He turned the photograph face up so that Gina could see it.

"Familiar?"

Gina shook her head. Borley placed his fingers over both sides, cropping the picture to reveal only the building and the two large figures in the foreground.

"That's it," said Gina. "That's my dream."

Chapter Five

◆

DOLINGEN PULLED HER thick black hair into a ponytail as she watched the one named Kate Lyons move along the busy avenue. Kate usually stopped at every store window, her mind utterly fascinated by the baubles inside. But today she walked briskly past the beauty parlor where she had her weekly manicure and entered a travel agency. Dolingen attached a bogus name tag and an artificial flower to the lapel of her red smock. Then she followed.

Dolingen found Kate standing at a wall display for a place called Cape Cod. Two life-size cardboard figures, both with hair the same ridiculous color as Kate's, jumped out of Styrofoam water and proclaimed that they were having fun. Dolingen moved closer.

"Do you know anything about the Cape?" Dolingen said when the moment seemed proper. She picked a Hyannis motel guide from the rack. Kate had the same one tucked under her arm.

"A little," said Kate. "I occasionally travel there on business."

"It must be nice to go to such exciting places on business."

"The Cape isn't that exciting."

"It is when all you see is the inside of a department store," said Dolingen. "Some of the girls are planning to go and I'm supposed to make the arrangements. Is it a good place for a vacation?"

"A long weekend is fine," said Kate. "Any longer and I would go batty. It's so quiet."

"Quiet is just what I'm looking for," said Dolingen. "Could you help me with reservations?"

"I don't work here."

"I'm sorry," said Dolingen. "I thought you did."

"Try her." Kate pointed to a desk where a young female travel agent was confirming a man's airline reservations over the telephone. "I use her all the time."

"Thank you. I'll browse a little first," said Dolingen. She turned back to the display. Kate touched her arm.

"Do I know you?"

"I doubt it."

"For a moment there I thought you looked familiar. I guess we both made a mistake. Sorry."

"No harm done," said Dolingen. "A lot of people think they know me. I guess I look like everyone's aunt."

"You don't look that old."

"I hide my age well," said Dolingen.

They stared at each other in silence. The man thanked the travel agent and headed toward the door.

"I better attend to business," said Kate. "Have a nice vacation."

"I'm sure I will," said Dolingen. "I hope your business works out."

Kate smiled weakly.

Dolingen turned back to the meaningless brochures as Kate introduced herself to the agent. She listened to every word they said.

Chapter Six

———◆———

AT DUSK, DOLINGEN stood at a public telephone one block from the basement apartment rented by Kate Lyons and her husband. The marriage was insignificant. She knew what husbands loved, what they hated, what could spark jealousy or unreasonable rage. Marty Lyons had been handsome and popular in high school, but he was a financial failure saddled with a beautiful and lazy dreamer. He would be no match.

Dolingen dialed their number. Marty answered.

"Hello," she said. "This is the Crow's Nest in Provincetown calling about your reservation for next week."

"You have the wrong number," said Marty.

"Isn't this the Lyons's residence? I'm calling for Kate Lyons."

"It's for you," said Marty.

There was a long pause. Kate's voice was cautious. "Yes?"

"Hello, Ms. Lyons. I'm calling about your reservation for next week. I'm afraid there has been an accident in the bungalow, a fire to be exact, and we must cancel your reservation."

"Okay."

"We have something for you the following week if you like."

In the background, Marty spoke sharply.

"No," said Kate. "That won't be necessary. Thank you."

The receiver clicked. Dolingen glided through the gathering dark to the house. She parted shrubbery and settled near a basement window. Kate was slumped over a kitchen table littered with a half-eaten meal. Marty loomed over her, working his hands into fists.

"Come on, Kate, how stupid do you think I am?"

"Oh, all right," said Kate. "I had a reservation for next week. I thought that while you were away I would go up there and look for a job."

"A job? On Cape Cod?"

"Well the job might not exactly be on Cape Cod. It's a good place to get discovered."

"Still dreaming, huh?" said Marty.

"It's not a dream," Kate insisted. "A lot of stars got their start on Cape Cod."

"Like who?"

"Lots of stars."

"I'm sure they had talent, whoever they are."

"Hey, I have talent, too."

"This is great. We're up to our ears in bills and you refuse to look for a job so that you can go up to Cape Cod and be discovered."

"I'm not going. The bungalow I reserved burned down and they can't give me a room next week."

"What a tragedy for the world of entertainment." Marty stormed to the door.

"Where are you going?" said Kate.

"Out," said Marty. "And when I get back from Houston next week, you'd better have a job. Because the next time I walk out this door, I'm not coming back."

Kate left the kitchen, then returned to the table with a hair brush in hand. Dolingen heard Marty's car start. So did Kate. She slapped the dinner dishes to the floor, then brushed furiously as if trying to scrape the artificial color from her hair.

Dolingen slid away from the window. It was a pity Kate Lyons had become so emotional. In a week, neither her dreams nor this argument would matter.

Chapter Seven

———◆———

BORLEY RECEIVED NO additional responses to his ad that day and decided Gina's dream of faceless parents was more promising than Kate's dream of stardom. He called Karen and told her he would be working late that night. Her noncommittal answer dripped with suspicion.

At dusk, Borley dialed Gina's number. The phone rang four times before she answered. He hung up immediately. He was ashamed to play phone games with a skittish woman, but he could think of no other way to determine whether she was home.

After stopping at a deli for coffee and a sandwich, Borley drove slowly past Gina's house. It was located on a hill overlooking a new town house complex. No car was visible in the darkened driveway, but lights burned in every second floor window. He made a U-turn and found a parking space half a block away. One of the upstairs lights went off. He turned off the Starion's engine. The street was busy enough so that he would not be obvious.

Borley ate his sandwich, drank his coffee, and tried to feel hard-boiled. He noticed three days of the *New York Times* still in blue plastic bags at the bottom of the driveway. Gina was not keeping up on current events. Another upstairs light went out. He prepared himself for a chase, but twenty minutes went by without any further activity. The sandwich balled in his stomach; the coffee ran through him.

He was doodling an invention to help real detectives on much longer stakeouts when a car turned into Gina's driveway and sounded its horn. Another window darkened, then Gina appeared on the porch. She hurried down a long stairway and climbed into the waiting car. Borley fired up the Starion.

The car led him to Playland, an amusement park that harked back to the 1920s with its art deco towers and bright primary colors. The park was enjoying renewed popularity after a long period of poor attendance and several suspicious fires. Signs boasted three space-age rides, new food concessions, and a refurbished boardwalk.

Borley parked two rows away from the other car. Gina emerged first, wearing the same stiff jeans she had worn that afternoon. Her companion was a young woman dressed in yellow. They entered the midway, where Gina cut a somber figure in the midst of happy children with their parents in tow. The woman in yellow took Gina's arm and tried to inject some spunk into her walk, but the result was an aimless shuffle through the crowd. Finally, she guided Gina to a bench.

Borley stood near a popcorn vendor. The woman talked earnestly and, from her gestures, seemed to be lecturing. Gina nodded mechanically at intervals, her eyes fixed on the ground. After several minutes, the woman stopped talking. Gina smiled faintly and accepted a sisterly kiss on the cheek. Borley followed cautiously as they headed down the flower-lined promenade to the boardwalk. Suddenly, Gina stopped. Her friend pulled, but Gina dug her heels into the ground.

"I'm not in the mood to meet anyone," said Gina.

"It won't hurt," her friend replied. She yanked Gina off her feet and did not release her arm until they reached the boardwalk.

Borley crossed to an unoccupied telescope. The cool boardwalk air was a mix of many smells— salt, wood, cotton candy. In the distance, the Whitestone and Throgs Neck bridges twinkled like diamond necklaces on a black satin pillow.

Gina and her friend leaned against the rail several yards away. Two young men approached them and struck up a conversation. Gina's friend did most of the talking. One of the men clapped his hands and Gina's friend pushed away from the rail. The other man motioned Gina to follow, but Gina simply shrugged. Her friend waved and the three disappeared into the crowded promenade. Gina did not watch them go.

She stood motionless with her hands on the rail and her eyes fixed on the water. Borley put a quarter into the telescope and swept the dark sound where ghostly boats rode the gentle chop. The field brightened as the far end of the boardwalk swung into view. He kept the telescope on Gina for only a moment, long enough to see a tear hurry down her cheek.

The lens cover fell with a click. When Borley stepped away, Gina was no longer at the rail. He ran to the entrance to the promenade, but did not see her. He hurried around a fountain and a miniature-golf course, but did not cross her path. He stopped. The boardwalk was crowded and every woman seemed to be wearing jeans. Then he noticed her walking quickly toward the end of the boardwalk. Just before she disappeared, she broke into a run.

Borley covered the distance quickly. The boardwalk ended at an unlit field used for firework displays and daytime helicopter landings. He stepped into the shadows and let his eyes adjust to the dark. The clanging rides and screaming children sounded far away. Across the field was a grove of trees. He moved cautiously, hoping to catch a movement against the distant lights on the water, but he saw nothing. Then he heard a snort. He held his breath, trying to get a fix on the noise. There was another snort, followed by a long whine.

He moved from tree to tree until Gina's white

blouse became visible. She sat on a picnic table with her head down and her arms wrapped around her stomach. She seemed to cry for hours. Borley became tired and shifted his weight. A twig cracked under his foot. The crying stopped.

"Who's there?"

Borley froze. Gina jumped off the table.

"Who's there?"

He knew she could not see him. She backed away slowly, then turned and ran across the field.

Borley did not follow. He hopped the fence at the far end of the picnic area and worked his way around the park to his car. He needed a professional's help.

Chapter Eight

———◆———

DOLINGEN REACHED Gina Lo Biasi's street minutes after the newspaper boy. She walked past the townhouses, noting the newspapers wrapped in blue plastic and the streaks of dew on the windshields of the idle cars. Four newspapers tattooed with muddy tire tracks lay at the bottom of Gina's driveway. Dolingen walked up the incline to the garage and wiped grime from an uncracked windowpane. Gina's beat-up car was inside.

The smell of gas wafted past her nose. She ran up the steps, across the back lawn, and past the gazebo. The smell was stronger. She forced open the back door and made straight for the kitchen. Gina, in a bathrobe, knelt with her head and shoulders propped on the open oven door.

"I've invested too much in you for this," said Dolingen. She slung Gina over her shoulder and carried her out onto the patio. Gina's breathing was raspy. Dolingen laid her on the picnic table and blew air into her lungs. Gina gagged, then fell into an even breathing pattern. Dolingen went inside. She shut off the gas, turned on the exhaust fan above the stove, and opened every window in the kitchen.

As the air cleared, Dolingen prepared a pot of coffee and kept watch over Gina's unconscious form. Ralph Lo Biasi should have been the perfect match. He was an egotistical man with a good career who could provide a comfortable life and protect Gina from harm without watching her every move. The marriage had worked well until the discovery of Gina's sterility. His reaction had been the big miscalculation, but Dolingen still expected Gina to endure. This immaturity annoyed her.

The coffee finished perking. Dolingen brought Gina inside and propped her up at the kitchen table. Gina's nose twitched and her eyelids loosened.

"Hi," Gina said weakly when her eyes focused. "Who are you?"

"No one," said Dolingen.

"Musta fallen asleep," said Gina. She sniffed the air. "What's that smell?"

"Coffee."

"Right. I was putting a pot on. Want some?" Gina tried to stand, but Dolingen stopped her.

"I'll get it," she said.

"I was having a bad dream," Gina said as Dolingen fixed a cup of coffee. "I couldn't breathe. I was scared."

"It was only a dream," said Dolingen. She handed the cup to Gina.

"Aren't you having any?" said Gina.

"No."

"My life is all screwed up."

"Yes, but do not worry."

"It'll get better?"

Dolingen nodded and slowly backed away toward the door. When she left, Gina was staring into space.

Chapter Nine

———◆———

BORLEY JUDGED Paul Savage to be about his own age. Savage had a walrus mustache and gray hair teased to cover a bald spot. He was too big to fit comfortably in the chair, so he leaned forward with his elbows on his knees.

"You mentioned something over the telephone about locating a missing person," said Savage.

"That's not exactly the case," said Borley.

"Mind telling me exactly what is the case."

"I want you to watch someone," said Borley. "A woman named Gina Lo Biasi."

"Who is she? A wife? A girlfriend?"

"Just someone I want watched."

"Mind telling me why?" said Savage. There was a sarcastic tone in his voice, as if he already had decided he did not want the job and needed to know more only to confirm his decision.

"I think that something may happen to her."

Savage tore open a brown nylon wallet and flipped a business card across the desk.

"I don't provide protection."

Borley looked at the card. It resembled a photographic negative with white fingerprints and lettering on a dark background. The services listed did not include protection.

"This is surveillance," said Borley. "I simply want to know what she does and where she goes."

"What is this thing you expect to happen to her?"

"I think she may disappear."

"Do you mean vanish into thin air or skip town?"

"I don't know," said Borley. "That's why I need her watched. I've already tried to follow her myself. I'm no good at it."

"It takes ability," said Savage. He pulled a handkerchief from a cavernous pocket in his leisure-suit pants and wiped his brow. "What makes you think that this woman is going to skip, and why do you care?"

"She's a participant in a psychological study I've been conducting," said Borley. "Her actions and present state of mind fit the profile of other participants who have skipped, as you say."

"So you want me to watch her nonstop until she does," said Savage. The sarcasm returned to his voice. He stuffed the handkerchief back into his pocket. "Forget it. I'm a one-man show. Call someone else."

"It isn't quite so involved," said Borley. "My information is that she'll disappear sometime between now and the first of September, most likely between dusk and midnight. You'll only need to watch her for a few hours at a stretch."

Savage settled back into the chair as much as his bulk would allow.

"What is the nature of your information?" he said.

"Data I have collected over the years. The specifics aren't important." Borley wrote Gina's name and address on a piece of paper. "She lives in a big Tudor house in a neighborhood that's busy enough so you won't stick out. I didn't. She's tall, thin, and has dark hair. She's about thirty but looks older. She has a husband, but he won't pose a problem. You'll only see him if he comes to rob the place."

Savage screwed his face into a question mark.

"He's in the process of furnishing his own apartment," said Borley.

"Good candidate to skip," said Savage. He explained his rates. Borley paid the retainer with the remaining bills in the petty cash fund and covered the shortfall out of his own wallet.

As soon as Savage left, Borley's phone rang. A woman introduced herself as Nicole Bourne. She was responding to his ad. Borley asked his litany of questions and decided he wanted to see her.

"I've never taken part in a psychological study before," she said. "I think it could be fun."

After thirty years of living with these disappearances, fun was not a word that leaped into Borley's mind. He set up an appointment for one o'clock that afternoon and turned his attention to department work.

Nicole simply appeared in the doorway while he was hunched over a pile of lesson plans on his desk. A cough pulled his eyes from the papers. They hit Nicole and stuck fast.

She had long dark hair parted in the middle and a round face with high cheekbones. Her arms and shoulders were sunburned. Light playing through her pink cotton sundress showed long legs and a narrow waist. One hand held a wide-brimmed straw hat. The other steadied a purse that dangled from her shoulder.

"Professor Share?"

He stood quickly without pushing back his chair and banged his knees against the desk. The metal echoed, but he ignored the sound and the pain shooting down his legs.

"Yes," he said as he walked around the desk. He took her hand. It was real. "It's not a mistake. You are Nicole Bourne?"

"Why would there be a mistake?"

"Two separate thoughts," Borley said, recovering his composure. "It's not a mistake that I am Borley Share and you are Nicole Bourne."

He moved a chair for her to sit, and went back behind his desk.

"I'm not a counselor," he said. "You would be surprised how many people think I am dispensing therapy."

"Have you received many calls?"

"Lately, yes." Borley opened his top drawer and quickly glanced at the photograph of Valerie. He had not forgotten her features. He simply needed to confirm his senses. The woman across the desk could pass for Valerie's twin. He closed the drawer. Two of them staring at him were too much.

"Interesting fantasies?" said Nicole.

"Some are, some aren't." Borley wrote her name, address, and telephone number on the label of a blank cassette. Then he explained that he was interested in hearing about the childhood fantasy first. They would discuss the recurrences later.

"Two instances leap to mind immediately," said Nicole. "The first is very old. It may have been a dream, or simply a trivial incident embellished over time. In my personal mythology, I think of it as my earliest memory. It took place in the old house upstate."

"Where upstate?"

"Interlaken. It's north of Ithaca. It started with me surrounded by light, like a bright fog. The fog slowly cleared and turned into a shaft of sunlight filled with dust motes. I was in a room. The walls were stark white with no decoration of any kind.

The floor was a shiny hardwood. The entire room was bare. There was no sound, but as soon as I stepped out of the light I could hear birds chirping and my mother singing while she cleaned another room in the house. Is this any help?"

"More than you can imagine," said Borley. "It's certainly the most artistic fantasy I've heard."

"The other instance was less artistic. I was a girl of about eight. It was before my father was transferred to his company's New York City office, so we were still living in Interlaken. I was sitting on the back steps one night, looking up at the stars, when I had something that I can only describe as an involuntary thought. It occurred to me that I had developed from a zygote that had been implanted in my mother's womb. Of course, I didn't think in terms of zygote and womb, but the meaning was the same."

"What do you mean by an involuntary thought?" said Borley.

"It's a clumsy phrase," said Nicole. "I wasn't thinking of anything in particular. As I looked up at the stars, the idea just struck me, as if a voice whispered into my ear. That was the official beginning of my adoption fantasy. It became stronger when we moved down here to Milton."

A tiny beep sounded and she glanced down at her watch.

"Damn, I knew this would happen," she said.

"What's the problem?"

"I've been running late all day and now I'm late for an appointment."

Borley motioned toward the phone.

"There are certain people you do not call," said Nicole.

Borley turned off the tape recorder. "That's unfortunate."

"Does this mean I can't be part of your study? I have a lot more to tell."

"I want to hear it," said Borley. "Tomorrow's Sunday. Are you free Monday?"

"I'm free until Labor Day," said Nicole.

"Then be here Monday afternoon."

"Thank you, Professor Share." Nicole stood and hiked her bag onto her shoulder.

"Borley. This isn't a class."

"All right, Borley." Nicole smiled and left the room soundlessly.

Borley waited, then walked down the corridor to the nearest window. Nicole crossed the sunny parking lot to a blue BMW 318. Borley watched until it left the parking lot and disappeared into the trees. Then he went back into the office and sat with his head tilted back, looking at the ceiling. The patterns in the acoustic tiles seemed to move, forming grotesque faces then dissolving into confusion.

"It's her, it's her, it's her," he breathed.

Chapter Ten

———◆———

NICOLE PAUSED BEFORE ringing the doorbell and turned toward the front lawn. The lush grass resembled a golf fairway. The short evergreens were perfect cones. The manicured flowerbeds exploded with zinnias and petunias. She pressed the doorbell. A few seconds later, Cassie answered with a wooden spoon in her meaty fist.

"Hello, Cassie. I hope I'm not late for Hugh."

"You can never be late for him, Miz Nicole." Cassie led her into the foyer. "That man's been runnin' me ragged. Up at six every morning. He's in the sunroom, 'less he's been runnin' around again."

Cassie waddled off. Nicole tiptoed through a large dining room and peeked into the sunroom. Hugh was draped across his favorite couch and was reading from a pile of magazines on the coffee table. One skinny leg dangled over the arm of the couch and an old deck-shoe slapped rhythmically against his heel. He flipped his reading glasses over his forehead.

"Well if it isn't my little girl," he said with a smile. He jackknifed to his feet and greeted her with a kiss and a fatherly embrace.

"How have you been, Hugh?"

"How have I been? Just look." Hugh backed away and struck a bodybuilder's pose. The baggy sleeves of his Chinese robe fell back to reveal skinny arms with thick veins. "I had a complete physical examination yesterday. You'll be happy to know the doctor said I might live forever."

"I don't think you have Cassie convinced," said Nicole.

"That woman will go to an early grave with all her worrying about me," said Hugh. He motioned for Nicole to join him on the couch.

"What are you doing with all these magazines?" Nicole said.

"Most of the stuff I've been reading lately is terrible, so I was thinking of doing some writing myself."

"What will you write?"

"I'm open to suggestion," said Hugh. "Do you think I'm expert enough to write about anything?"

"Oh, stop being so modest," said Nicole, gently punching his arm.

"Before we do anything else, I have something to show you," said Hugh.

They climbed to a small attic room filled with cardboard boxes. The heat had weakened the fiber until each was ready to burst. As Hugh rummaged through the boxes, Nicole wiped away some dust from a tiny window for a better view of the lawn.

"It's hard to believe that a piece of land could be so intimidating," she said.

Hugh was elbow deep in a box and did not look up.

"I was never very tough as a boy, so I rather enjoyed being thought of as a monster," he said. "Aha! Here we have it."

Hugh straightened up as much as the low ceiling would allow. In his hands was an antique sextant.

"I don't believe it," said Nicole. "Where did you find it?"

"I was moving these boxes the other day and there it was. Remember how to work it?"

Nicole gently took the sextant from Hugh's hands.

"Of course I do," she said as she sighted it out the window. "You once said I was the only sixth grader in the whole state who could navigate by the stars."

"Yes, but you forget the hell of a time I had convincing you to try it. Remember the story I told you?"

"Something about how the earliest astronomers were really sailors."

"Right," said Hugh. "You wanted to become an astronomer then, or was it an astrophysicist?"

"Astronomer," said Nicole. "Funny. Rory invited me to watch a meteor shower the other night."

"Who's Rory?" said Hugh.

"Someone I met back in the spring. A professor and a poet. A fairly good one, too, from what I hear. But not for me."

"Still catching them and throwing them back, eh?" Hugh winked. "How was it?"

"I told him I was busy, but the truth was I didn't want to go. I couldn't see myself sitting out in some field and looking up in the sky for fleeting specks of light. Have I changed that much?"

"Don't worry," said Hugh. "You'll come back to it."

"That's not the question," said Nicole.

"Ah, but it's the answer. Most people think that growing up means they must rid themselves of the things that gave them real enjoyment as children. Only the chosen few make livelihoods out of their childhood pleasures."

"Like the shipbuilder who sailed paper boats in gutters after rainstorms," said Nicole.

"It has never ceased to be fun."

"Should I go back to school to study astronomy?"

"Heavens no!" said Hugh. "But when the urge to look up at the sky strikes you, do it. With or without this Rory."

"Funny you should call it an urge to look up at the sky. I had three interviews that day and was so tired when I returned home, I fell asleep on the couch. I woke up about midnight feeling very anxious. I undressed and mixed a drink, but the anxiety just got worse."

"That isn't like you," said Hugh.

"I know. No matter what's on my mind, my sleep's never disturbed. But it was this time. I heated up some milk. Imagine me drinking warm milk?"

"Don't knock it," said Hugh.

"Then, instead of drinking it in bed like a normal insomniac, I took it to the window. Of course, it couldn't be any window, so I moved a table in the living room and pulled up a chair. Minutes later, that huge fireball appeared and, funny thing, I was not even surprised. I fell asleep with my arms on the windowsill."

"Warm milk works every time."

"I didn't touch the milk," said Nicole. "And when I woke up I still felt anxious."

"Which is why you called."

Nicole handed back the sextant and sat as best she could on the windowsill.

"You have heard the name Malcolm Engel, right?" she said.

"I have, but I can't remember the context."

"Well, he is a well-known securities lawyer and he has just offered me a job."

"Sounds like a good career move," said Hugh. "What's the problem?"

"The problem is, I don't know why he made the offer."

"No mystery. You're quick, intelligent, you cut a good pose, you made law review. Your marketability should be sky high."

Nicole turned toward the window.

"I also had an affair with him," she said.

Hugh let out a whistle. "You always were attracted to older men."

"It was back when I was a freshman in college," Nicole said. "Remember my first trip to Florida, the one you encouraged me to take? I met Malcolm on the beach at Fort Lauderdale. He was attending a symposium. We talked for a while and he invited me to a cocktail party. I never dreamed our paths would cross again."

"I could say a lot of things about irony at this moment," said Hugh.

"Malcolm has had me to three interviews and

two expensive dinners with different partners. He
needs a decision by the end of the month because
he is scheduled to fly to Tokyo after Labor Day.
He wants the new associate to accompany him."

"An awful hard sell," said Hugh.

"This is exactly the job I want," she said. "But
if I take it, I will always wonder whether the offer
was based on my ability or that week we spent in
Florida."

Out in the bushes beyond the lawn, Dolingen
rolled up a portable listening device she used for
eavesdropping. She had listened to many such
conversations between Nicole and the man called
Hugh Michael Elliott in the years after she had
arranged the transfer of Charles Bourne to his
company's New York office. She knew Elliott
would advise against accepting the offer and she
knew Nicole would obey.

Dolingen pushed through the bushes and
walked quickly along the neighboring lawn to the
spot where her own vehicle was parked. Nicole
was the last one on the list. It was time to begin.

Chapter Eleven

———◆———

GARNO EMERGED WHERE the waters of the inlet lapped gently against the remains of a tumbledown seawall. He could have taken the tunnel and come up in the basement of Dolingen's quarters, but he knew that he should breathe the air, put the balance back in his ears, and stiffen the jelly in his inactive legs. The path wound up a hill covered with trees and choked with thick underbrush. Broken glass and rusted cans littered the damp ground. He pulled a bottle from a thorn bush. The thin film at the bottom had the unmistakable smell of alcohol. He tucked it under his cape and moved on.

Garno was completely acclimated by the time he broke out of the trees behind the stone building. He walked around its perimeter, carefully noting every window and corner, every surface and angle. Dolingen met him at the front door and they embraced briefly. She had aged during his journey. The signs were barely perceptible, but at close range he could detect tiny crinkles around her eyes and a loss of luster in her raven hair.

Dolingen led him through an octagonal foyer with a marble floor and crystal chandelier. The parlor had a picture-window facing east. The sun was appreciably higher now and cast a warm trapezoid of light on the red carpet. Garno placed his hands on the windowsill. The air was hazy and turned the water of the inlet into a slab of dull glass. A tiny boat sliced across the surface.

"How have the children fared?" he said.

"Fine," said Dolingen. "The rate of attrition has been unusually low and I have succeeded in keeping them within a tight geographical range."

"Are there any entanglements?"

"Nothing significant. The marriages are weak. The friendships are matters of convenience."

"Has the one we left behind caused any problems?"

"None whatsoever. She has abided by our agreement. I would know otherwise."

"That is fortunate," said Garno. "I have had my worries."

"I can assure you," said Dolingen. "She fears detection as much as we do."

Garno turned away from the window.

"I was surprised that your signal directed me here," he said. "You have moved far from our usual sites."

Dolingen motioned him into the foyer, where she opened the brass gate of a tiny elevator. She pressed a button. A motor whirred, gears engaged with a snap, and the elevator slowly rose to the top of the mansion's tower. The sky was white and the hot sun cast no shadows. More of the inlet was visible and along its shore several other mansions rose above the treetops. Dolingen pointed to a shroud on the horizon. Below it was a cluster of many buildings.

"That is the city called New York," she said. "It is the largest, most sophisticated city in this part of the world, and it attracts people by the thousands every day. The children have not been immune. Soon after your last visit, I realized the futility of preventing a migration from our usual rural areas. I bought this estate and gradually arranged for each of the children to relocate here. Although communications systems are especially advanced and theoretically jeopardize our secrecy, I have found that in highly populated regions such as New York we may continue to operate without fear of detection."

"What about this?" said Garno. He pulled the bottle from his cape. "This is fresh and there are many more like it."

"This property is the traditional gathering place for the young people of the community. They come here at night to drink alcohol and explore each other in primitive ways. I occasionally set the police on them."

"The police, young people, this building. You are calling entirely too much attention to yourself."

"You exaggerate the danger," said Dolingen. "I contribute generously to police charities. They answer my calls and ask no questions."

"When were they last here?"

"The night you arrived. They broke up a group that had come to watch the meteor shower. The young people do not return for weeks after I call the police. You will be long gone and I will have this property on the market by then."

"No doubt to purchase a more elaborate one."

"I have sacrificed much by remaining here," said Dolingen. "I do not consider this mansion to be a selfish indulgence. I chose this particular estate because it fulfilled our specifications. And at this time of year, fog rolls off the water every night. It was especially thick the night you arrived."

"I hope you are correct," said Garno.

"I am. I know these people better than I care to." Dolingen opened the elevator's gate. "Are you completely established?"

"Yes. All prepared. The bedrock here is solid, but the tunnel is now complete," said Garno.

"Then shall we renew ourselves?"

"It has been a long time."

"A long time for me, too," she said.

"You mean you have not met someone here who might understand our ways?"

"I thought I found someone once," said Dolingen. A smile crossed her face. "I met a man while I was observing one of the children. He seemed different, but when we came back here he touched me in his primitive way. I fought him off long enough to lower the screen. At first, he was interested. Then he became frightened and tried to run. Of course, I could not allow him to leave."

They rode the elevator down to the second floor. Dolingen's room was bright with the sun and was sparsely furnished. The bed was a box spring and a mattress covered by a plain white sheet.

As Garno watched Dolingen unhook the curtains and plunge the room into artificial twilight, he thought about the man she had brought here. What excitement he must have felt when he saw this full-bodied Dolingen, this Amazon—there was no other word in the language for her—climb out of her gown and lie on the bed. What promises waited to be fulfilled as never before. What a fool the man had been to run.

Dolingen, naked, stretched out on one side of the bed. Garno returned from his reverie, removed his clothes, and joined her. A screen descended from the ceiling, settling lightly between them. The screen was longer than they were tall and about half as high. It was not quite opaque, but in the dim light of the room they were invisible to each other.

Garno rolled onto his back and lifted his hands. A mist emanated from the screen and gathered over him. Slowly, the mist resolved into shapes, and in a moment Dolingen was straddling him. The breasts he cupped in each hand felt as firm and as substantial as the breasts of the real Dolingen who lay on the other side of the screen.

Chapter Twelve

"YOU'RE BECOMING ANNOYING," said Karen. She was still in her bathrobe, sitting sideways at the table with sections of the Sunday *New York Times* scattered around her.

Borley stopped in the middle of the kitchen and arched his back.

"That nerve is acting up again," he said.

"Then see someone."

"You know how I feel about doctors."

Karen returned her attention to the Book Review. Borley straightened his back as soon as he left the kitchen. He picked up the hall telephone and carried it into the living room. He looked at his watch. Five minutes had passed since he last checked the answering machine at his office.

The tape was silent. He replaced the phone and went out to the front steps. Heat from the sun radiated off the concrete walk. If his back really did hurt, the heat would feel good. Instead, he felt stifled. Sundays were such useless days even in the best of times. Today was worse. Savage was tailing Gina, no new women were likely to respond to his ad, and Nicole was not scheduled to appear at his office until tomorrow. It was going to be a long day.

Karen came outside and settled next to him. She was wearing a short, cotton dress and sandals. Her tan legs looked hard in the bright daylight.

"Aren't you getting ready?" she said.

"What should I wear?" said Borley. He had no idea where they were going.

"I doubt it will snow," said Karen.

Borley was glad he did not ask. He changed into jeans and a golf shirt. When he came outside, Karen was sitting in her car with the motor running. She did not criticize his outfit. Maybe he would remember their destination as she drove.

They arrived at a field below the Kensico Dam, where an open-air jazz concert was just getting underway. Karen had mentioned it several weeks ago. Time certainly had flown.

Borley sat Indian style on the grass with Karen nestled between his legs. He welcomed the music. He could move his head and snap his fingers and Karen would never guess he was thinking about the disappearances. In all his years of study and his recent search for likely candidates, he never expected to find anyone like Nicole Bourne. His entire theory was predicated on an undetected chemical process that manifested itself as the adoption fantasy. Now he had the perfect control, a woman who not only had a recurrence of the fantasy, but who also walked, talked, and looked like Valerie. Savage would observe the others. He would keep Nicole for himself.

At intermission, Borley told Karen he had to find a men's room. He crossed the field, walked into the village, and found a telephone booth at a gas station. There was a message from Savage on the office answering machine. Borley dialed the number he left.

"She doesn't do anything," Savage said about Gina. "She hasn't gone anywhere, no one's visited. All I do is watch lights go on and off in the house."

"What do you suggest?"

"I suggest that you're wasting your money."

"All right," said Borley. "Switch over to someone else."

He gave Savage Kate Lyons's name and address.

"What's the book on her?" said Savage.

"Housewife with delusions of grandeur," said Borley. "I promise that she'll make for more interesting watching."

"Let's hope," said Savage.

They hung up, and Borley checked his machine for additional messages. There was another beep.

"Hi, Borley. This is Nicole. Something's come up. Is three o'clock convenient tomorrow? I'm looking forward to seeing you."

Borley ran all the way back to the field.

Chapter Thirteen

IT WAS THE middle of the night shift, and fluorescent lights hummed in the empty corridors of St. Catherine's Hospital. Garno and Dolingen strode confidently through the lobby and waved at a tired nurse sitting at the reception desk. The nurse ignored them; they were dressed in hospital whites.

The elevator took them to the fifth floor. In Room 516, Elizabeth Donahue lay in fetal position. Tubes from her nose led to a respirator. Tubes from her arms led to intravenous units. Wires from her head and chest led to brain and heart monitors, which beeped in alternating cadence. Elizabeth's face was mashed into the mattress inches from the nightstand, where family photographs stood in simple wooden frames.

Dolingen let the door close and leaned back against it. Garno slowly approached the bed and rolled up his sleeves.

"How did this happen?" said Garno.

"An automobile accident," said Dolingen. "Three years ago. She is completely paralyzed but refuses to die."

Garno brushed his knuckles on Elizabeth's hard cheek.

"The Donahues are wealthy and converted a room in their house so Elizabeth could be with them," continued Dolingen. "I prevented the transfer by inducing a seizure. The doctors now refuse to discharge her."

"She will linger for many years," said Garno. "Many more years than these doctors can imagine. Beyond the Donahues, perhaps beyond you."

Dolingen joined him at the bedside. They looked in silence at the woman contorted below them. Elizabeth's head moved slightly.

"She senses your presence," said Dolingen.

"They all have sensed me," said Garno. He lifted his eyes. "Someone's coming."

He disappeared into the bathroom. Dolingen wiped her hands on her smock. Footsteps approached rapidly in the corridor. She unhooked the chart from the foot of the bed and pretended to be reading the monitors. Seconds later, the door opened.

"Who are you?" said a young nurse.

"Private duty," said Dolingen.

"I know the Donahues very well. They didn't say anything to me about a private-duty nurse."

"Well I'm not here because I want to be."

"I'll take that." The nurse swiped the chart out of Dolingen's hands.

"You're not the only person in the world who can read monitors." Dolingen wrenched the chart back.

A shaft of light escaped from the bathroom.

"We'll see about this," said the nurse.

She started to turn. Garno shot out his arm and flicked his fingers on the bone behind her ear. Dolingen caught her before she hit the floor. Garno motioned toward the bathroom.

Dolingen pulled down the nurse's white panty hose and sat her on the toilet. She returned to find Garno at the bedside. Elizabeth struggled to lift her head. Her eyelids fluttered and her mouth moved, but no sound came out. Garno spoke softly. His hands left the rail and moved slowly, inexorably, toward the broken woman. One hand cradled the back of her skull; the other bridged her temples. His power surged. The machines fell silent and the green line of the brain monitor went flat.

Chapter Fourteen

SAVAGE WAS DRINKING his first cup of coffee when Kate Lyons came out of her house. Her hair was permed to look like a mane. Her thighs broke through a pale yellow dress. Savage thought the material was called chiffon. He knew it looked damn good on her.

Kate walked to a badly dented Toyota hatchback. The door opened with a dull snap, and the motor hesitated before turning over. Savage slipped his Plymouth into gear without recapping his container of coffee. He did not expect a high-speed chase.

Kate drove to White Plains and parked in a municipal lot on the edge of the business district. Savage found a space but stayed seated as she strolled through the parked cars. When he got a fix on her general direction, he opened his door wide and used both hands to pull himself upright. It was a hot day. He hoped Kate did not have much walking in mind.

Kate went through a pedestrian tunnel leading to Mamaroneck Avenue. Savage gave her a good lead. She turned left and was still visible when Savage reached the sidewalk, a trail of turned heads in her wake.

Half a block from the tunnel, Kate entered a building. Savage picked up his pace. The door to the building was glass with ACME EMPLOYMENT AGENCY lettered in white. A gold plate for a CPA was fastened to the stonework next to the door.

Inside, Savage could see a small hallway with a staircase.

Savage wrote the address and the time in his notebook. Then he bought a newspaper, lit a cigarette, and pretended to wait for a bus. He did not have to pretend for very long. Kate was back on the sidewalk within five minutes. Savage stubbed out his cigarette.

Kate walked past the pedestrian tunnel and went into Macy's. Savage had worked in the store's security division before he decided to start his own investigative agency. He was not proud of the many years he had spent watching for shoplifters through peepholes in the walls and he had not returned since the day he quit. But Kate was inside, and there were too many different exits for him to wait on the sidewalk. He hoped no one would recognize him.

Kate browsed through cosmetics and jewelry while Savage sauntered behind. Four different salespersons asked if he needed any help. He told them he was just looking, thanks. Then he cursed Borley Share. Kate moved into lingerie, and Savage imagined her in skimpy things. It was interesting work.

After an hour, Savage followed Kate out through the same door she had entered. She walked down Main Street and turned into another building. Savage waited for a minute, then went as far as the foyer. The building directory listed three law firms, a funding company, a hokey-sounding import firm, and an employment agency. A pattern was developing: Kate was looking for a job. Savage noted the name and went back out to the sidewalk. Kate was not far behind. Another pattern was developing: Kate was not having much success.

She then walked into three stores in quick succession. Each store had only one entrance, so Savage could amuse himself on the sidewalk while Kate was inside. Two slices of pizza and one Italian ice later, Savage was trailing her back through the pedestrian tunnel. Her dress looked limp and the spring had gone out of her step.

Savage reached his car before Kate reached hers. He was about to start the engine when he noticed her walking back across the lot as if something had attracted her attention. He squinted through the reflections on his windshield. A tall woman dressed in a nurse's uniform stood at the far end of the lot.

Savage had a camera under the front seat. He quickly attached a telephoto lens and balanced the camera on the roof of the car. The nurse was tall and had her black hair woven into a single thick braid. Savage focused on them in profile. They were speaking in a strangely intimate way that made him feel uncomfortable. He squeezed off a shot. The nurse turned, almost as if she had heard the shutter click from across the parking lot. He squeezed another shot, this time of her entire face.

The nurse turned back to Kate and spoke. Kate nodded vigorously. The nurse patted her shoulder, then went off in the direction of the tunnel. Kate stared after her for a minute, then walked briskly out the back exit of the lot. Savage threw his camera into the car. He ran to keep her in sight.

Kate moved like a woman with a mission. Display windows did not exist, pedestrians jumped out of her path. Without slowing down, she made a sharp turn into a frozen yogurt shop. The glass front was tinted, but Savage could see Kate's dress receding into the dimness in the rear. He wiped the sweat from his face with his handkerchief. The shop looked like a dead end, so there was no reason to follow her inside. He sat on a nearby bench, opened his notebook, and wrote the address of the shop and the time. He expected the nurse to arrive, but she did not appear.

Fifteen minutes passed. Savage paced in front of the entrance but could not see Kate through the tinted glass. He returned to the bench and watched several people enter and leave. After another fifteen minutes, he could wait no longer.

The inside of the yogurt shop was icy. A skinny man with a thin beard and a pale complexion stood behind the counter. He raised his head as if to take an order, but Savage walked past the counter to a group of tables in the rear. A few people were scattered about, one to a table. Kate was not one of them. Savage went back to the counter.

"Yes," said the man. He had either a lisp or an affect. Savage would have bet affect.

"I'm looking for a blond woman wearing a fancy dress," he said.

"So?" said the man.

"She came in here a half hour ago. I don't see her now."

"Maybe she left," said the man.

Savage leaned over the counter and flashed his license and a badge that could pass for a police shield.

"I'm hot and I'm tired and I don't like yogurt. She walked in, but she didn't walk out."

"Okay, okay," said the man. "I saw the one you mean. She went into the back, talked to someone, then came up here and ordered a coconut bang."

"Who was the someone?"

"A man, about your height, but—"

"But skinnier, right?" said Savage.

"You know him?"

"No, but I hear it a lot."

The man backed away as if Savage would hit him. Savage looked around the shop.

"I don't see either of them," he said.

"Honestly, I don't know where they are. I work this shift by myself," said the man. He seemed angry about it, as if Savage was another in a long line of accusers. "I can't see everyone. I told the boss, I can't—"

"Is there a back door?" said Savage. He did not wait for an answer. He left the man whining about his simply impossible job and found the door himself. It opened onto a municipal parking lot. Kate was nowhere in sight.

Savage went back to the counter. The man was serving a customer, but his eyes darted Savage's way. Savage furrowed his brow and jerked his thumb. The man left the customer.

"Who was here first, the man or the woman?"

"The man, I think."

"What was he wearing?"

"A white linen two piece suit and a blue satin shirt. I didn't notice his shoes."

Savage wrote the description in his notebook.

"Surprised you didn't notice him leave," he said.

The man looked puzzled. Savage left him yammering about his simply impossible boss. The hot air hit Savage like a sledgehammer. He trudged back to the parking lot. Kate's Toyota was still in its space. The meter showed less than ten minutes remaining. Obviously, she had not planned on staying in White Plains for very long.

Savage walked over to his own car and waited for the ten minutes to run out. He had a strange feeling that what he had seen, or not seen, was just the kind of flaky thing Borley Share was talking about. He had the names of two employment agencies, a nurse on film, and a description of a man who had walked out of a coffee advertisement. He started his car. Borley Share knew more than he was telling.

Chapter Fifteen

◆

"I WAS ALWAYS tall for my age," said Nicole.

Borley slowly withdrew his hand from the tape recorder. The cassette spun silently.

"When we moved to Milton, my parents enrolled me in a Catholic school. It was run by nuns and they constantly played the girls off against the boys. In the classroom, we were their pets. In the schoolyard, the boys got even. We would play tag, keep away, all those games, and the boys were very rough. But there was one girl they couldn't handle." She smiled. "I was the fastest runner in the class.

"I walked to school every day with three other girls. Milton isn't a town made up of straight streets and square blocks. The roads curve and the property lines look like pieces of a jigsaw puzzle. The girls had a route mapped out that took a series of shortcuts across people's lawns. We were careful to avoid flower beds and newly planted grass, so no one seemed to mind. Right in the middle, exactly halfway between my house and the school, was a lawn bordered by a low stone wall. It didn't look any different from the others. It had shrubs and flower beds and nice green grass that sloped up to an ivy-covered house. But the girls wouldn't cut across it. They told me it was haunted. I asked who would haunt such a nice yard and they described men who sounded like Italian gardeners. Weeks passed with us walking on the sidewalk and not seeing

anything on that lawn except an occasional bird.
I tried to convince them we should cross, but they
refused. Finally, one Friday morning, I decided I
was going by myself. After all, I was the fastest
runner in the class. I jumped onto the stone wall,
waved goodbye, and ran across.

"It was easy. I sat panting on the far wall and
looked back at my footprints in the dew. No one
jumped out of the bushes. No one shouted from
the house. I was breathing evenly by the time my
friends reached me. They couldn't believe I had
done it.

"The crossing became a daily event and my au-
dience made me bold. Sometimes I would loop
around trees. Other times I would walk for long
stretches and stare at the house. Once I even did
a cartwheel. No bogeyman bothered me, until the
day I was alone.

"It was a Saturday and I was going nowhere in
particular. I trotted across the lawn and watched
the sun reflect off the windows of the house one
by one. Suddenly, someone grabbed me.

"He wasn't a bogeyman. My first thought was
that he was my grandfather or someone who
could be my grandfather because he was tall and
skinny and so was I. He had mussed white hair
and wore a yellow cardigan that hung on him like
a sail.

"'The man of the house will be happy that I
caught you,' he said. He turned me around and
marched me into the house, straight to a large
kitchen. All I remember were thousands of pots
hanging from the ceiling and the biggest black
woman I ever saw. He told her to watch me until

he called the boss. She smiled, then made a fist the size of a beachball around a wooden spoon. I wasn't going anywhere.

"Ten minutes later, he returned wearing a red silk smoking jacket instead of the yellow cardigan. It looked like a sail, too. He introduced himself as Hugh Michael Elliott. He owned the place.

"He told me that he had been watching me for several weeks. He actually did not mind children taking the shortcut, but if he didn't prevent them the lawn would turn into a playground. So he promoted the idea of the bogeyman. He said no one had dared to cross his lawn in years. Then I came along. He liked my boldness, especially the cartwheel. He said he had to meet me.

"He took me into a large room, his great hall, as he called it. I'll never forget my first sight of that room. I thought I was in a castle. Pennants hung from a cathedral ceiling and moved gently in the air. Sunlight streamed in through stained-glass windows. My feet sank in a Persian carpet as thick as a mattress. I was ten years old and didn't think that people lived like that. I still have problems with the idea.

"Hugh sat me down in a large velvet chair and pulled a gold cord that hung near the wall. Then he asked a simple question. 'Nicole, what do you want to be?'

"You must realize, even as a girl I had this need to be the best. If I hadn't been born a fast runner, I would have become one just to beat all the boys. Now picture me with a wealthy ship-builder in a room that looked like a castle with models of the ships he had built set up like religious statuary. What was I going to be? I was going to be famous.

"He laughed, but didn't say anything because Cassie the maid rolled in a cart with milk for me, tea for Hugh, and cookies for both of us. It was only years later that I realized how seriously he took me. He told me I could come over anytime I wanted and he would tell me stories. However, I could no longer cross his lawn. It looked bad.

"That was the start of a twenty year friendship. In case you haven't guessed already, Hugh was the person I couldn't be late to see on Saturday."

"Do you visit him often?" said Borley.

"Not as often as I should," said Nicole. "Lately it seems I only visit him when I need something. I feel a little guilty about that."

"What did you need this time?"

"Just help in making one of the biggest decisions of my life. I refused a job offer."

"A good job?" said Borley.

"A great job. Exactly what I am looking for in a career. Money, travel, high-class clientele. I have worked hard to become a lawyer and I expect to be well compensated for my effort."

"You must have had a good reason to refuse."

"I once had an affair with the senior partner, so I always would have suspected his reason for hiring me. Still, the job was tempting. But talking to Hugh made me realize there are other jobs." She smiled. "Other men, too."

"I see," said Borley. "How did your parents react to Hugh?"

"I didn't tell them about him at first," said Nicole. "I would get home from school, change out of my uniform, and run over to his house. If Hugh was there, he would tell me stories about cruises and safaris, about meeting H. G. Wells in a London club. If he wasn't there, he would leave a book with Cassie for me to read. I would stay there until dinner, then run home.

"One day, my mother was waiting for me on the porch. She had been driving past Hugh's house and had seen me coming out. I told her everything about this wonderful man and the exciting stories he told me in the room that looked like a castle and how he was going to help me become famous. She walked to the far end of the porch and gazed up into the big swamp maple that covered the house and said, 'If this man really wants to help you, let him. Only don't tell your father.'"

The telephone rang. Borley switched off the tape recorder and answered. It was Savage.

"I got to see you right away, Share. Something's happened."

Borley looked at Nicole. She was staring at his diplomas. He turned toward the window with his hand cupped over the receiver. Then he realized he looked suspicious and turned back. Nicole, being very polite, now concentrated on translating small print Greek.

"Yes?"

"I mean something happened to this Kate Lyons."

"What?"

"I don't know, goddammit, but you and I have to talk."

"Now?"

"Of course now," said Savage. "I'm at the White Plains Diner."

Savage hung up. Borley rattled the receiver onto the cradle and hid his hands under the desk. They were shaking.

"I never would take you for your age," said Nicole as she pulled away from Borley's diplomas.

"I'm afraid that I am," said Borley.

"Isn't it odd how people use the word afraid?" Nicole returned to her chair. "They often mean regret rather than fear."

"I regret that I am."

"Don't regret it," said Nicole. She held his eye for a long moment.

"I also regret that something has come up," said Borley. He really meant fear. "We'll have to cut this session short and resume at another time."

"How is Wednesday?"

"Deal," said Borley.

Nicole reached across the desk and they shook hands. "Maybe one day we'll get through everything."

She let her hand trail slowly out of his. Then she was gone.

Chapter Sixteen

———◆———

BORLEY FOUND SAVAGE in the first booth by the diner's entrance. A powder-blue jacket dangled from a hook. There were dark half-moons of sweat in the armpits. Savage mopped his brow with a wrinkled napkin and flicked cigarette ashes into an empty coffee mug.

"You surprise me, Share," said Savage. "From your attitude on the phone I thought you'd take your sweet time."

"I was with someone when you called. What happened?"

"You are going to tell me what happened," said Savage. "And if you don't come clean right now, you'll be looking for another investigator."

"Kate disappeared, right?" said Borley.

Savage gave him a long, even stare. Then he nodded solemnly.

"Shit," said Borley. He smacked the table. He was right. The disappearances were starting, and right on time. He smacked the table again and resisted the impulse to laugh. "How did it happen?"

Savage started with the visit to the first employment agency. Borley confirmed that finding a job had become a serious issue between Kate and her husband. Savage told him of the hour spent in Macy's, then mentioned the nurse in the parking lot.

"Something funny was going on between the two of them," said Savage. "I definitely got the feeling that they knew each other for a long time. It was no casual meeting."

"And after that Kate started to run?"

"Not exactly run, but she hustled. I haven't moved that fast in years." Savage continued with the half hour spent outside the yogurt shop and the description of the man seen with Kate inside. "It'll make more sense if I show you."

Borley shrugged. "Sitting here isn't doing us any good."

Savage drove back to the parking lot. The sun, already turning red as it moved from afternoon to dusk, hung above the buildings and cast long shadows across the empty spaces. Kate's Toyota was alone in the middle with an overtime sticker under a wiper. Savage parked and stood with his arm on the open door. Borley quickly circled the Toyota and returned. Savage leaned into his car and pushed the dashboard lighter.

"Yogurt shop's right around the corner," he said. "Fella I talked to might still be working."

"Forget it," said Borley. "I don't think he can help us anymore."

The cigarette lighter popped. Savage lit up and took a long drag.

"You know, I can't figure you, Share. First you say you don't really know these women, but somehow you're worried they're going to disappear. So you hire me to watch them. Sure enough, one of them does disappear. I can't figure out how, and you treat it like nothing happened. You don't want to go to the cops. You don't want to hear my story about the nurse or talk to the man in the yogurt shop. If I could figure out a motive, I'd think you were involved."

Borley took a deep breath. "Look, I didn't want Kate to disappear. But now that she has, I might as well tell you the rest."

Chapter Seventeen

———◆———

"IT STARTED THIRTY years ago," said Borley. They were in his office in the Humanities Building. Borley sat with his feet on the desk. Savage settled comfortably in a chair wheeled in from an adjoining office. A band of pink clouds floated above the horizon. "I was a student at Cornell, taking summer courses between my freshman and sophomore years. One day, while walking across a bridge to campus, I ran into a woman. Literally. I must have been looking down into the gorge because I bumped right into her. She dropped some papers. I tried to help her, but she gathered her papers together and ran away.

"A few nights later, I noticed her sitting alone in a local bar. She waved me over like a long lost friend. She apologized for her rudeness on the bridge and explained she had been late for an appointment.

"Her name was Valerie Kennedy. We started

dating. It was nothing like a fifties movie, but it was nothing very involved, either. I was living in a dorm, she was renting a farmhouse outside of town. I was only eighteen and she was somewhat older. I didn't ask. Her age was intimidating.

"In early July, Valerie invited me to the farmhouse for the first time. I took a bus to the last stop at the south end of town, then walked a mile up a dirt road to an old dairy farm. The owner supported himself by letting a local power company run wires across his land and by renting the farmhouse to Valerie.

"We sat on the front porch swing, drinking beer and watching the fields turn blue. She admitted to me she was twenty nine, almost thirty. I told her it made no difference to me. She led me upstairs to a narrow room with a map of New York State plastered to the wall and a small daybed. We became lovers."

"Let me guess," said Savage. "She was your first."

"One of those facts that won't be important, you'll see," said Borley. "We saw a lot of each other after that. You could say that I moved in. After about a week, I noticed she never spoke about her past, her family, what she did for a living. So I asked her. She wasn't very candid."

"Skeleton in the closet?" said Savage.

"Not exactly. She told me about her parents in five words. They died in an accident. Then she took me upstairs to a room I had never seen. It was filled with pictures."

"Artist, eh?" said Savage. He smiled as if that explained everything.

"Pretty good one, too," Borley said defensively. "All the pictures were bird prints except for two. One was a sketch of a woman Valerie knew. The other was this."

Borley handed over the photo of *American Gothic 2100 A.D.* Savage raised one eyebrow as if the strange figures explained even more.

"In the days following that conversation, Valerie started to talk about a future together. She wanted to get married. Of course, I never had considered marrying anyone before, but I was comfortable with the idea of spending the rest of my life with her. I was happy. It didn't last long.

"The bad stuff started on August second. I woke up in the middle of the night and found her on the floor, curled up in the fetal position. I leaned down to wake her and saw she was sucking her thumb. I couldn't believe it. I shook her and slapped her hand from her mouth. She half opened her eyes and said, 'I'm sirsty.'

"I got a glass of water. She drank it in loud gulps and fell right back to sleep. I didn't. The next morning, she denied anything had happened. I tried to convince her, but she screamed and stamped her feet like a petulant child. I couldn't deal with it, so I went up to campus.

"I returned at dusk and heard yelling when I was still on the road. It sounded like someone was being murdered. I ran up to the porch and saw that she was in the kitchen. She had four chairs in a line in front of the oven. She was shaking a finger and yelling at a figure in one of the chairs. I moved closer, so I could see. The figure was a doll.

"She called the doll Baby Valerie and demanded to know where the doll had heard something. She seemed to listen to an answer, then flew into a rage. 'Again! You said it again, you brazen child!' she screamed. She slapped the doll off the chair. I ran in and grabbed her in a bear hug. She bucked like crazy. I rode her across the kitchen and pinned her against the sink. She sobbed, 'She doesn't believe she's mine! She doesn't believe it!' until she went limp.

"I put her to bed. She slept fitfully for a while then woke up and told me she had always believed she had been adopted. She would look at pictures of her parents, grandparents, aunts, uncles, cousins and tell herself she wasn't one of them. She searched for a birth certificate, hospital records, adoption papers, but never found any proof. All she had was the feeling that she was different. She withdrew from her parents, and in her own words, consciously found it in herself not to love them.

"Then in high school she met a woman who encouraged her to draw wildlife prints. At first, Valerie thought that her talent was further proof of her unknown lineage, but as she became more successful she also became more tolerant of her family. They never became close. There wasn't time. Her parents started talking about moving to Virginia. Valerie didn't want to go because she was afraid the move would end her art career. She refused to accompany them on a trip to look for a house. As they drove away, she shouted that she never had loved them. Those were the last words she ever said to them."

"Some heavy guilt," said Savage. He seemed more sympathetic to the story than he had before.

"The catharsis helped," said Borley. "The next day she was the same bouncy Valerie I had bumped into on the bridge. The final exam for my summer course was that day. She walked me down to the bus stop and promised to have a special dinner waiting that evening.

"I missed my usual bus and didn't reach the farmhouse until dusk. Dinner was on the stove, but Valerie wasn't around. I looked in the backyard. I looked in her upstairs studio. I waited on the porch until well after dark. I never saw her again."

Borley took a photograph from a file folder and pushed it across the desk. It showed a woman with dark hair, high cheekbones, crinkled eyes, and a smile of wry amusement.

"Pretty woman," said Savage. "What steps did you take to find her?"

"Everything I could think of, but nothing helped. The police said it was not the first time she had run off, and it probably would not be the last. After all, she was an artist. I became so angry at their lack of concern that I demanded to be arrested on suspicion of kidnapping. The desk sergeant laughed. The people at the Missing Persons Bureau were nicer, but no more helpful.

"For months it seemed I did nothing but review that entire summer like a movie in slow motion. I decided she had been trying to tell me something, right from the moment we had crashed into each other on the bridge, and it had been my failing not to see it.

"The following May, I was paging through back issues of the *New York Times* as part of a research assignment. I came across this."

Borley handed Savage a small piece of newsprint yellowed with age. He leaned back while Savage read silently.

VANISHED AT LA GUARDIA

NEW YORK, August 6 (AP)—Police are investigating the disappearance of a woman who was last seen disembarking from a DC 3 on the runway of La Guardia Airport at approximately 8:00 last evening. Mary Ann Fitzgerald, 29, of Syracuse, had flown to New York to visit friends. The plane landed on time and the friends, Toby and Cindy Cole of Queens, said that they saw Miss Fitzgerald emerge from the plane and walk down the steps onto the runway. They waved to each other, then the Coles left the observation deck and headed toward the gate. They told police that Miss Fitzgerald did not pass through the gate and never appeared to claim her baggage. Miss Fitzgerald's father, Hiram, also of Syracuse, arrived in New York today to claim his daughter's personal belongings and to help the police in their search.

"I went to see Mr. Fitzgerald," said Borley. "He told me that just before his daughter disappeared she reverted to juvenile behavior and demanded to know whether she was adopted."

"Sort of like your Valerie," said Savage.

"Not exactly, but close enough," said Borley. "I had a hunch and started sifting through old missing-persons reports. I found ninety two cases involving women approximately thirty years old. Each one had neurotic tendencies and suddenly experienced the recurrence of a childhood adoption fantasy, then disappeared. By that time I was in graduate school. I wanted to do my thesis on the disappearances, but my advisor wouldn't let me. He said I would never get my doctorate that way."

"Obviously you didn't just forget about them," said Savage.

"Right," said Borley. "I kept searching and I found a total of three hundred seventeen cases."

"All disappeared at once?"

"No, that's the interesting part. The disappearances occur at thirty-year intervals. I plotted the last group, which included Valerie, on a map and found the center to be just outside Auburn, New York, at the northern end of Lake Cayuga. Thirty years before that, the disappearances formed a semicircle with a point on Lake Ontario just west of Rochester as its focus. Thirty years before that, the same thing occurred around Erie, Pennsylvania."

"I'm not sure what you're driving at," said Savage.

"Neither am I," said Borley. "I admit my study has been rather low rent as studies go. The pattern in the data is clear, but the factors are a complete mystery. Basically, I believe the answer is chemical. The behavior of the women—the adoption fantasy, the reversion to childish behavior—is an outward manifestation of the physiological process. These women are chemically programmed to disappear."

"What about the pattern?" said Savage.

"My theory is that an external stimulus sets the process in motion and the woman goes off, like a sick cat, never to be seen again. The trouble is, I haven't been able to identify a stimulus that occurs in thirty year cycles over such a small geographic area."

"So where did you come up with Kate Lyons and Gina Lo Biasi?" said Savage.

"Part educated-guess, part luck," said Borley. "I'm not here by accident. There has been an eastward trend in the centers of the disappearances, so I picked this area as the next likely stop. With this being the thirtieth year, I ran an ad for a psychological study. The participants must have experienced a recurrence of a childhood adoption fantasy. Many people answered, but Kate and Gina were the only two who exhibited all the symptoms."

"And you tried to follow them, decided you couldn't handle it, and called me," said Savage.

Borley nodded.

"Not that it would have mattered, but even if you had given me this background at the start, what did you expect me to do?"

"Follow them to wherever they went," said Borley. "This way I could find them, test them, and identify the stimulus."

Savage stood and hitched up his pants.

"I don't like your whole theory," he said. "It's

too scientific. Now, I know you're a scientist and I'm just an old dick who likes to eat and spends too much time sitting on my ass, but you begin to get a feeling about things after a while. You begin to realize that people do things for very simple reasons and that the fancy theories are just that, fancy theories."

"You think these are kidnappings," said Borley.

Savage smirked as if Borley were a slow pupil who had just grasped a fundamental idea.

"That is the one explanation I find totally preposterous," said Borley. "I have records of disappearances that go back ninety years, a hundred twenty if I want to stretch some of the data. That's almost the Civil War."

"You didn't see the way she talked to that nurse," said Savage.

"The way you talk about it, I wish I had."

"I think I can help you there," said Savage.

Chapter Eighteen

———◆———

DOLINGEN DROVE SLOWLY down a block of row houses and found a parking space beneath a darkened streetlight. In the back of the van, Garno removed his silk shirt and linen pants.

"What is proper?" He passed his hand over several boxes of outfits. Dolingen indicated a white cotton shirt with a button-down collar and gray slacks.

"Her name is Betty Simpson." Dolingen consulted a file card attached to a clipboard. "She works as a secretary for an insurance company. She has been nervous about her future because her recent attempts at a promotion have failed."

"Today her troubles are over," said Garno. He stepped over the inert form of Kate Lyons and squeezed into the front seat. "How do I reach her?"

"She recently joined a computer dating service. The files were easy to invade. You are her first date, Mr. Scott Bradley."

"Very well," said Garno.

"Betty is considered plain and dull. Her best friends are her two cats." Dolingen pointed to Kate. "She wanted to believe you were a talent scout, but Betty may be suspicious of you."

Garno climbed the stairs to number 213 and rang the doorbell. Footsteps approached on a bare floor, and a muffled voice said, "Behave." The door opened.

"Hi, I'm Scott."

Betty wore a red dress that was recognizably out of style. Their eyes met and the smile dropped from her lips. One hand moved to her throat, the other remained frozen to the doorknob. Behind her, the cats scurried into hiding.

"May I come in?" said Garno.

"Sorry, yes," said Betty, coming out of her fog. She led him down an unadorned hallway into a small living room.

"Where do you feel like going for dinner?" said Betty. She took a hesitant step toward the couch then played with a ruffle on her dress.

"I'm not familiar with Queens, so I thought you could suggest a place," said Garno.

"I don't know of too many places around here," said Betty.

"We can sit and talk for a while," said Garno. "This is my first computer date."

"Mine, too," said Betty. She dropped the ruffle. "I'll get some wine."

She hurried into the kitchen. Garno looked around the living room. A small television shared a coffee table with a pile of crossword puzzle magazines and photographs of Betty's two cats. Curtains hung from crooked rods. Nail heads pushed out of the plasterboard walls.

There was a loud crash in the kitchen. Garno found Betty kneeling amid shards of glass. She shook her head in embarrassment.

"That's me. Old Butterfingers."

"Careful you don't cut yourself." Garno knelt beside her.

"Don't worry, I have a lot of practice with this." She flinched. "Oh no. I think I just did."

"Stay right there," said Garno. He wet a paper towel and gently dabbed the cut. Betty kept her eyes fixed on her hand, which was lost in his palm. "Don't want you to bleed to death on our first date."

"You're very kind," said Betty.

They returned to the living room and Garno poured the wine.

"I hope you like it," said Betty. "It's from Yugo-slavia."

"I'm sure it is good," said Garno.

They clinked glasses and sipped.

"What do you do?" said Betty.

"I'm in personnel."

"I tried to get a job in our personnel department. They gave it to another girl, though. It must be very interesting."

"The job makes one very good at reading people," said Garno. "There is nothing to be nervous about."

"I'm not nervous," said Betty. She squirmed deeper into the seat cushion and clasped her hands together. "Well, maybe a little."

Garno carefully took her hand. At his touch, she jumped farther away.

"I'm sorry," she said.

"It takes awhile," said Garno. This time she allowed him to take her hand. "See? Nothing to be afraid of. How's that cut?"

Betty opened her mouth to answer, but the words stuck in her throat. Garno reached for her chin and gently turned her head so that she was facing him. She looked into his eyes for a moment, then broke away.

"Where are my cats?" She stood up. "Thor, Pippin, where are you?"

"They must be here somewhere," said Garno.

"Thor, Pippin, come here." She walked across the room.

"Betty, please sit down." Garno patted the couch, but Betty ignored him.

"Something is wrong. Thor! Pippin!"

She looked under the chairs and behind the bookcase.

"You did it," she said angrily. "You scared them."

"Betty, please," said Garno.

"You scared them."

She ran out of the room, her voice echoing as she searched wildly around her apartment. Garno found her in the bedroom. She had pulled a dresser away from the wall and was kneeling behind it.

"There you are," she said to the cats.

Garno walked to the window and drew the curtains. Betty lifted her head above the dresser.

"What are you doing?" she said.

Garno clenched his fists and felt the power oscillating along his spine. He turned toward Betty. A look of terror crossed her face. He took a step as she struggled to dislodge herself from the tight spot behind the dresser.

"What are you doing?" she said as she scrambled to her feet.

Garno said nothing. The power shot out of his arm and knocked her into the hallway. She crawled along the wall until she reached the bathroom. She tumbled inside and kicked the door shut. Garno heard her struggling to turn the latch. He blasted open the door. Betty scrambled under the sink, one hand clutching her throat, the other waving in vain against the power of his eyes.

"One more step and I'll scream," said Betty.

Garno crossed the threshold.

"One more step and I'll scream." Her voice weakened.

He loomed over her.

"One more step and I'll—"

He touched her neck.

Chapter Nineteen

———◆———

SAVAGE LIVED ON the bottom floor of a two family house in an apartment that reeked of bachelorhood. Junk mail and old newspapers covered the kitchen table. Huge cotton shirts dangled from cabinet handles in a futile attempt to hang out wrinkles. Empty bottles and cans choked a crevice between the stove and the refrigerator. An entire section of the wall was bare plywood. It did not seem out of place.

"I don't spend much time here," said Savage. He flung his jacket over the back of a chair. "Beer?"

Borley did not answer.

"Why the hell not?" said Savage. He took two bottles from the refrigerator and threw their caps into a paper bag. "It's not every day that we have a bona fide mystery on our hands."

Borley took a swig and mumbled in agreement. Savage finished off his beer in three long pulls and added the bottle to the pile of empties.

"And now to work," he said. He opened a flimsy door in the plywood wall. "Might as well take a look. We both can't fit in here."

The door was lined with black felt. The room behind the plywood was as neat as the kitchen was sloppy. An L-shaped workbench ran along two walls. Three shallow pans were arranged in a precise line next to a small aluminum basin sunk into the bench. Measuring cylinders stood in size places on a shelf. A small window was blotted with plywood and trimmed with more black felt. In the corner was an enlarger.

"Guy I knew did the pipes so I could have running water," said Savage. "I did the rest myself. You're welcome to another beer when you're ready."

Savage shut himself in and switched on a loud extractor fan. Borley walked over to a window and raised the shade. A smudge of moon drifted over the rooftop across the street.

"Can I use your phone?"

"Sure," yelled Savage. "There's one on the wall there, another in the bedroom if you want privacy."

Borley chose the wall phone and punched in Gina's number. She answered on a seventh ring with a voice that expected bad news. Borley hung up.

"No one home, eh?" said Savage.

"She was home."

"Great conversationalist, Share."

"How the hell do you know?"

"These walls are lightproof, not soundproof."

"It was Gina," said Borley. "I was checking to see if she was all right."

"Detection at its finest."

"I'm not proud," said Borley. "The woman has enough troubles."

"Forget it," said Savage. "I pull the same shit sometimes."

"At least she's still around," said Borley. He moved closer to the plywood wall. "Are you a photography buff?"

"You mean the darkroom?" said Savage. "Never used to be. But there was someone in my life who was. I built it for her."

Savage was silent for a moment. Borley leaned against the wall.

"Don't lean against the wall," said Savage.

Borley jumped away. "What happened?"

"Then she wasn't in my life anymore."

"Did she disappear?" Borley hoped the humor he intended passed through the plywood.

"Nothing so mysterious," said Savage. "She ran off with another guy."

"I'm sorry to hear that."

"Don't be. Those things happen. I ended up with a darkroom and I got out of Macy's."

"Macy's?"

"I used to work their security. I almost shit when Kate Lyons went in there today and I had to follow. You know there are catwalks behind the walls?"

"I didn't know," said Borley.

"And there are guys pacing those catwalks and looking through peepholes onto the selling floors," said Savage. "I guess she didn't see herself marrying a store detective. Hell, I wasn't even that. I was a glorified Peeping Tom."

There was another long silence. Borley strained his ears to hear if Savage was concentrating on a complicated part of the developing process. He heard nothing except the big man's labored breathing.

"It was rough for a while, after she went off, I mean," Savage finally said. " I had the darkroom half done and decided to finish it anyway. I had some crazy idea that she'd come back. She didn't. Then I decided to become a photographer myself. I'd have my stuff in *Life* magazine and really show her. I was going to do flowers and birds and old people in the park. But I found that the pictures I saw in my head never came out on film.

"One night I was in here hanging some sorry prints up to dry and I decided, fuck it, I'll never be a photographer, but I goddam wasn't going to be a glorified Peeping Tom for the rest of my life. I quit Macy's the next day and opened up the agency."

"How long ago was that?"

"Ten, eleven years," said Savage. "You remember my business cards? I did them myself."

"Very clever," said Borley. He took another beer from the refrigerator and cleared a spot on the table. He wanted to call Gina again, but he knew it would frighten her. He could identify himself and explain that he was following up on last week's interview. She might buy it, she might not.

"How much longer?" said Borley.

"Not much."

"Do I have time to run past Gina's?"

"Believe me, this is more important," said Savage.

Borley rooted through the newspapers and found the most recent was last Thursday's. There was a story about the meteor and a poor photograph of the luminous trail that had hung over the area long into the night. The story said that the object, part of that annual Perseid meteor shower, had been the size of a Volkswagen and had exploded over the Long Island Sound. The Volkswagen image struck Borley as odd. Why not a Toyota, or a Chevy, or a small Mercedes? Why not simply say it was a four-by-six-by-eight-foot chunk of iron that entered the atmosphere at such a speed that it completely vaporized before reaching the ground? Even he knew that much about meteors.

Savage unlatched the plywood door. His shirt was completely soaked and his hair was plastered to his bald spot. He elbowed a pile of newspapers to the floor and laid a print on the table.

"It's small and it's not washed, but it's a good likeness," he said.

Borley placed his thumbs on either side of the print and moved his eyes closer. "Do you have a magnifying glass?"

"First thing I bought when I became a detective," said Savage. He produced one from a silverware drawer.

Borley inspected the print, moving the glass from top to bottom, side to side.

"I don't believe it," he said.

"Know her?" said Savage.

"Not exactly, but remember I said Valerie did only two pieces of artwork that were not bird prints. One was that strange painting. The other was the sketch of a woman's face. She didn't wear a braid, but otherwise she could be the same woman."

Savage cleared more space and sat down, his elbows like two tree trunks on the table.

"This case just took an interesting turn," he said.

"Maybe."

"Cut the bullshit," said Savage. "You said Valerie knew the woman she sketched. What was their connection?"

"She was the woman who took an interest in Valerie and started her on her art career."

"What was her name?"

"Dolly something. I never met her."

"Isn't that odd?"

"Why would it be?"

"Because this Dolly must have been a very important person in Valerie's life. So were you. I'd expect she'd have wanted the two of you to meet."

"I was with Valerie a total of two months. There were a lot of people in her life I never met."

"Let's go back to the beginning," said Savage. "Why did Valerie draw the picture of Dolly?"

"She didn't specifically mean to do a picture of Dolly. The sketch was supposed to be a study for the face of the female figure in the painting. It came out resembling Dolly, and Valerie couldn't decide whether that was right."

"How did she mean 'right'?"

"Artistically right, I guess," said Borley. "I don't know. We didn't discuss it in depth."

Savage drummed his thick fingers on the table. Each hit with a thud.

"What steps did you take after Valerie disappeared?"

"I told you I went to the police and the Missing Persons Bureau. I took long walks around the farmhouse, looking for I don't know what. If I had money I would have hired a private investigator, but I didn't. The first break came when I found that newspaper article about the Fitzgerald disappearance."

"Did this Dolly go to the police or to the Missing Persons Bureau?"

"Not that I know of."

"Doesn't that seem strange?" said Savage. "Her best pupil disappears and she isn't concerned."

"Are you suggesting that Dolly was involved?"

Savage poked at the print. "I'm saying we have evidence that connects someone who looks like this with both Valerie and Kate. From a purely investigative point of view, we can't ignore it."

"I hired you to tail people, not to solve the mystery."

"I don't care why you hired me," said Savage.

Borley used the magnifying glass to study the face of the nurse. "But Dolly would be near seventy."

"That could be a bad picture, she could be made up, it could be a coincidence, I could be fucked up. Anything's possible, but nothing's any less likely than your theory of stimuluses and chemicals in the brain and women who act like sick cats."

Borley again looked at the face. His theory, concocted from newspaper accounts, missing person's reports, and interviews with batty old people, seemed to fly apart under Savage's scrutiny. But the disappearances were happening again, and for the first time he had someone who believed him and was willing to help.

"Whatever the reason," said Borley. "I want to uncover it. I don't want anyone else to go through what I've been through."

Savage smiled. "Don't bullshit me with idealism. Revenge ain't a bad reason."

"If you are right, I'll consider it," said Borley. "What's the next move?"

"Make some larger copies of that picture," said Savage. "I have some police contacts. They might know something. Then I'll stick on Gina's tail. I won't get fooled twice."

"Doesn't sound as if you'll need any direct help from me," said Borley.

"We'd just get in each other's way. I'll keep you posted if anything important happens," said Savage. He plunged his fist into a pocket and rattled some coins. "Remember the rates I quoted you? They don't apply anymore. All I want is expenses."

"All right," said Borley. "But why?"

Savage nodded toward the darkroom. "Consider it a favor from one hopeless romantic to another."

Chapter Twenty

———◆———

BORLEY ARRIVED HOME after midnight with a small manila envelope containing a clear four-by-seven photo of the nurse. The house was dark. He felt his way to the stairs and tiptoed up to the bedroom. Karen lay with her arms around a pillow and the sheet kicked into a pile under her feet. Late moonlight rippled across her thighs. Borley held his breath; Karen did not move. He walked quietly down the stairs and called his office answering machine. Savage reported that Gina was safe at home. He was quitting for the night and would resume at noon tomorrow.

Borley went out to the toolshed. He picked up the flashlight and, not bothering to close the door behind him, searched through the pile of bird prints for the charcoal sketch of Dolly. He had framed it himself, long ago in the brief period when he saw himself as a caretaker for Valerie's art rather than the chief investigator of her disappearance. He never had considered the sketch to be important. It certainly had not seemed as interesting as the colorful painting that loomed above him in the darkness beyond the flashlight's beam.

The sketch was near the bottom of the pile. He wiped dust from the edge of the frame and placed it on the dresser next to the photo Savage had given him. He played the beam on one, then the other. Each had thick dark hair, a small mouth, and high cheekbones that gave a vaguely Oriental look to her eyes. Dolly's face was a rendering by Valerie's subjective hand, while the nurse was a product of the camera's objective lens, but the similarities were remarkable.

"What's going on?"

Borley wheeled and flashed the beam at the voice. Karen stood in the doorway. She wore a short bathrobe cinched at the waist. Her small fists were on her narrow hips. Before Borley could speak, she walked past him to the dresser. He pointed the flashlight toward the floor, but enough light reflected around the room for her to see the two pictures.

"It looks like you have finally found a replacement," she said.

"What are you talking about?"

"You haven't had me fooled, Borley. I've known about your little dollhouse for a long time. It was weird, but I could live with it as long as it was a secret toy you took out only at night. But obviously I can't ignore it any longer."

"You don't understand." Borley used the flashlight like a teacher's pointer. "This person was a friend of Valerie. And this other one may be involved in a similar disappearance that happened today."

"I don't want to hear it," said Karen. "I've watched you and your investigation for years. Every year I thought it would go away, and every year it remained. I thought it was an obsession. Now I realize it is something worse, one colossal self-indulgence."

"You never listened. If you had, you would have realized that it wouldn't go away, not until after this summer. And I'm right, goddammit. A woman disappeared today." Borley held the flashlight on the photograph. The reflection obliterated the nurse's face. "*She* might know the answer."

Karen shook her head. She walked to the doorway and paused with her hand on the doorjamb.

"You always criticized me for never finishing anything," she said without turning around. "See how critical you feel tomorrow."

Borley watched her bathrobe fade into the darkness of the backyard. He switched off the flashlight and plunged onto the hard daybed mattress.

Borley slept deeply until well after ten the next morning. He went into the house and immediately sensed something was amiss. Karen's usual baseline level of noise—the click of the keyboard, the rattle of the printer, the hiss of the coffee pot —was absent. The silence was so total he could hear the electricity flowing through the wires.

The study looked as neat as a computer store. The walls were bare, the floor uncluttered, the surface of the desk visible for the first time in his memory. Upstairs, he found yawning closets full of empty hangers and a bed freshly made with an old set of his sheets. An airmail envelope was propped against the pillows. Inside was a note written in red marking pencil on computer paper. The strokes were bold, as if Karen had spent the night conceiving draft after draft until the words were correct.

Borley:
    I am now officially finished. Good luck with the
new doll you have found for your dollhouse.
                                        Karen

Borley crushed the note in his fist. She thought
he was crazy, pure and simple. If she could have
seen beyond her jealousy and impatience, she
would have realized that his self-indulgence was
irrelevant. Something had happened thirty years
ago and thirty years before that. Now it was happening again. He wasn't crazy. Confused and baf-
fled, maybe, but in a short time he would have
his answer.

Borley spent the afternoon moving his file cabinets from the shed into Karen's study.

Chapter Twenty-one

———◆———

BORLEY STOOD AT the entrance to the Humanities
Building with his tape recorder slung over his
shoulder. The sun had burned off the morning
cloud cover, and with it any hint of coolness.
Across the parking lot, the dark green trees were
as still as a painting. He plucked open another
shirt button.

Nicole's BMW appeared on the drive then cut

diagonally across the empty lot to a visitor's space close to the building. Borley quickly descended the stairs and met her before she left the car. She rolled down her window. Cool air laced with pleasantly mild perfume wafted past his face.

"So this is your machine," said Borley. He leaned into the window. She was driving barefoot.

"My baby." Nicole patted the steering wheel. "I'm banking on a prosperous future. Which one is yours?"

Borley pointed toward the Starion several spaces away.

"That's too baroque for me," said Nicole. "Besides, I heard it has a mind of its own."

"In what way?"

"Computers going haywire, the car not responding to the driver as if possessed. One of those car magazines had an article."

"I didn't read any reviews and I bought the car because I liked the name. It's a portmanteau word of star and Orion."

"Are you a hunter?"

"In a manner of speaking," said Borley. "Anyway, I've never had any trouble."

"I'll still take Europe over Japan," said Nicole. She stepped into her sandals and peeled her shorts from her legs. "Did you just drive in?"

"No. The air-conditioning unit is out, and the entire building doesn't have one window that opens."

"Say no more," said Nicole. "I'll trust you to find a shady place and a cool breeze."

The Humanities Building backed onto a field of baked grass. Beyond was a grove of trees. Borley cleared leaves and broken twigs from a rock that felt cool to the touch, and he invited Nicole to sit. Somewhere an unseen brook poured into a pool.

"I had a professor in law school who always tried to hold classes outside in the spring," said Nicole. "He was a liberal, so I guess he felt compelled."

Borley placed the tape recorder on the sloping face of the rock.

"Professors are like that," he said.

"I know. I'm an expert when it comes to professors. I've known several on a personal level along the way, and one thing I have learned is that no matter how soft-spoken and accommodating they might seem at first, they are basically pedantic. The classroom must bring it out."

"Not all professors are pedantic," said Borley.

"You're right," said Nicole. "Those who aren't have personality defects."

"I can't wait to hear which type I am."

"You don't seem to fit either," said Nicole.

"That is because you do all the talking."

"Well, let's hear you talk. Why are you doing this study?"

"Scientific interest, publish or perish, the academic rat race."

"Are you sure it isn't your way of meeting women?" said Nicole.

"I'm not a Svengali," said Borley. "Besides, I would have wanted to meet you anyway."

"Is the tape on?" said Nicole.

Borley reached for the tape recorder. Nicole laughed.

"I'm only kidding," she said. "About the Svengali, too."

"Maybe I will tape this," he said, but he put down the recorder.

"Honestly, Borley, is the air-conditioning working?"

"Yes, but not very well," he said. "Hell we're adults. After all these sessions I know much about your deep past and little about your present. I thought being out of the office would allow us to talk about something else."

"So I will talk about me and you will talk about you. That reminds me of sixth grade. The nun told us to write two pages about anything we wanted. I didn't know where to begin and turned in a blank paper. It was the only test I ever failed."

"I had nothing so structured in mind."

"Let's get right to the point," said Nicole. "You're interested and so am I. The fact is that I'm involved with someone right now. Not heavily involved and not for very much longer, but I handle my social life in a particular way. No entanglements. The breaks are clean, precise. When I walk, I don't look back.

"This has nothing to do with you, but I'm seeing this person for the last time tomorrow night. He's a professor." She smiled. "He doesn't know it will be our last date, but he won't be surprised. We have been at odds for a long time. He claims to be sensitive, but his words are implied contradictions. He tells me that if we were married I could have my career. Well, thanks a lot. As if my career is his to give."

"Sounds like a problem in semantics," said Borley.

"Right. The man is a poet. I assume he says what he means." She jumped off the rock and paced on the path. "I'm demanding, headstrong, and intolerant of weakness. Hugh's words, not mine. The problem is that Hugh is my yardstick, and few men can measure up. Now do you still want to see me?"

"Not until you're free," said Borley.

"Fine. Let's get started." Nicole leaned across the rock and, holding his arm for support, switched on the tape recorder.

"Do you remember where we left off?"

"Yes," said Nicole."

She told Borley her grammar-school class had contributed to the adoption of a South American baby by Jesuit missionaries. The idea of adoption had troubled her and she started rummaging through closets and drawers for proof of her own origin. Her voice melted into the sound of the brook. The rock dissolved beneath Borley and he sat suspended in time, hearing nothing and seeing nothing, until the rock reformed and her words again sharpened in his ears.

When the session was over they left the grove and made plans for dinner two nights later.

Chapter Twenty-two

———◆———

GINA SPENT SEVERAL days after Playland without once considering the mess her life had become. Each morning she retrieved the newspaper from the sidewalk and read it from beginning to end. Each afternoon, she wandered through shopping malls and idly compared the prices of items she never would buy. Each evening she ate alone in a dining room that was dark except for pinholes of sunlight coming through the trees covering the house. The break came on Wednesday. She rose from her uneaten beans and franks and walked around the table to the place she had dutifully set for Ralph. On the back of his empty chair, a blurry white circle danced with the breeze. She batted his place setting to the floor.

Her thoughts came in a rush. Everything her friends had told her spewed forth. She was not yet thirty. She was attractive. She had a lot to offer someone. The situation with Ralph was bad, but it would not last forever, and when it passed, life would be good again. Better. She had many years ahead of her. She had to keep her hand in life, enjoy herself, and be good to herself. She would not give Ralph the last laugh.

She held the back of Ralph's chair until the torrent passed and the last thought ebbed away, leaving her feeling calm, resolved. She dumped her food, plate and all, into the garbage receptacle under the kitchen sink. Then she bounced upstairs, reconnected the hall telephone, and dialed Alice.

"Anything wrong?" Alice said when she realized it was Gina. They had not spoken since Playland.

"I was wondering if you were doing anything tonight," said Gina.

"I was planning on that singles' dance the Shore Club holds every week," said Alice.

"That might be fun."

"Gina, did you hear what I said? I've asked you to go there the last three weeks."

"I know."

"Is this the same Gina who dragged me out of Playland the other night?"

"I don't think so. It might be a new Gina."

"Well, I'm not going to ask what changed your mind," said Alice. "How's eight-thirty?"

"Great." Gina clapped her hands. It was the perfect night for a new beginning.

Out on the street, Savage slouched behind the wheel of his Plymouth and chewed ice from a paper cup. He had been on the stakeout since early afternoon, breaking once to buy a sandwich and three containers of iced tea, then several times to waddle around the block to a service station. In another half hour the sky would be dark. He could use the nearby hedges.

Savage noticed lights go on in the upstairs rooms and a thin shadow move across drawn shades. It was unusual activity for a woman who seemed to spend her evenings sitting alone in a darkened house. He instinctively reached for his notebook, then remembered he was not interested in recording her movements or establishing a pattern. He simply had to keep watch, and not lose her.

Minutes passed without any further activity in the house. Savage pulled himself to the passenger side and threw open the door. The outside air was only slightly less humid. He arched his back and pulled his sweaty shirt away from his body. He hoped Gina planned another drive to Playland. He could use a nice ocean breeze.

Savage walked toward a dark house fronted by a tall stand of hedges. No pedestrians and no cars were in sight. He ducked behind the hedges and let loose, wishing he could think of something less diuretic than coffee or iced tea to drink on a stakeout. Just as he finished, he noticed a pair of headlights moving slowly down the street. He froze. The lights were moving slowly enough to be a patrol car. The last thing he needed was to be arrested for trespassing while on a stakeout.

The lights moved past. The vehicle was not a police car but a dark-colored van. Savage stepped out onto the sidewalk. The driver seemed to be looking for something, an unoccupied house, a lone pedestrian. The van stopped in front of Gina's house. Savage crouched next to his car. The passenger door of the van opened, and the interior light fell on a white hand. At that moment a car came down the street from the opposite direction and turned into Gina's driveway. The hand closed the door and the van shot away. Savage reached into his car for his notebook and wrote down the license number—177–ZHS. The letters meant the van was a rental.

A woman left the car and walked into the darkness at the end of the driveway. Savage climbed into his own car and pulled his camera from under the front seat. Lights went out in the second floor of the house. A few moments later the woman reappeared with Gina in the driveway. Savage aimed the telephoto lens. The image was dim but clear enough to satisfy him that Gina's caller was not the nurse.

The women drove down U.S. 1. Savage tailed them easily, enjoying the rush of wind into the stale air of the Plymouth. They turned into the Shore Club, a converted mansion that had failed as a restaurant and now served as a meeting hall. The parking lot was unlit and disordered. Savage found a space and watched as Gina and her friend walked toward the entrance. A table tended by three men in loud Hawaiian shirts was visible just inside the door. The two women handed over money, received leis around their necks, and went inside.

Savage stepped out of his car and lit a cigarette. Gina and her friend would be here for a while. He cut through the parking lot and walked down the road until he found a pay phone.

"It's nine o'clock," he told Borley's machine. "Gina and a woman friend are at a singles' dance at the Shore Club. I think this is the same woman you saw her with at Playland. I'll report again later."

* * *

Inside the Shore Club Gina stood next to a fake palm and worked the lei in her fingers. Beyond a wall of shadow, the heads of half a dozen couples bobbed in the speckled light of the dance floor. On a small stage a deejay pleaded with the rest of the crowd to join in. Gina turned toward the bar, where Alice was still waiting for their drinks.

A short, fat man materialized from the shadows and asked Gina to dance. She shook her head wildly, but the man persisted.

"I'm waiting for a friend," she said.

"Aren't we all." The man leered. He moved on.

Alice appeared with the drinks. "Having fun?"

"This may have been a mistake," said Gina.

"Why do you say that?"

"They all look like such losers."

"There are many different types of men in here," said Alice. "Some are funny looking, some strange, some nice, a few you might even call handsome. But remember, you didn't come here to meet the love of your life. You're here to learn how to meet people again, to be Gina, not Ralph's wife, in a social situation. I had to do it, too."

"But I don't know how," said Gina.

"Forget about your eyes, forget about your heart. Go with this." Alice patted Gina's stomach. "If you see someone and get a good feeling there, follow it. If not, have a dance and say thanks. You might be surprised by the end of the night."

The crowd was beginning to listen to the deejay. Gina drained her drink and followed Alice to the edge of the dance floor. The same fat man asked her to dance and this time she accepted. Neither the dance nor the man did anything for her stomach, so when the song changed she simply thanked him and returned to the shadows. She was not there long. Another man asked, then another. Soon she was smiling, laughing, touching, having the most fun in recent memory. An hour later, needing a break, she met Alice at the bar.

"You seem to be managing," said Alice. She handed Gina a drink.

"I haven't met Mr. Right, but who cares?"

"Glad you listened?"

"Yes," said Gina.

They clinked glasses then turned away from the bar to survey the dance floor. Gina noticed the man at that moment. He was tall and simply dressed—no shirt open to a bulging belly, no gold chains, no tight white deck pants accentuating his crotch—just a golf shirt and a pair of Levi's. He stood away from the crowd that ringed the dance floor and wore a look of detached amusement, as if he were a golfer from some distant fairway who had heard the music and, being curious, dropped in. She guessed his age to be about her own. His face, especially with the slight grin, looked boyish, but then a light played on him and she could see that his hair was flecked with gray. He edged closer to the dance floor and planted himself across from her. Gina stole a glance at Alice to see if she had noticed him as well, but Alice was checking out the crowd. Gina peeked back at him. His head moved slowly toward her until their eyes met and he smiled.

Gina nervously took a sip from her drink. Something in her stomach fluttered, then calmed. She looked again. The man was still staring at her, his serene smile at odds with the noise and movement around him. She nudged Alice.

"I think my gut is telling me something," she said out of the corner of her mouth. She could not take her eyes off the man.

"Really?" said Alice. "Where is he?"

"Straight across the room."

Alice picked the man out of the crowd. He definitely was staring back at Gina.

"That older man?"

"What do you think? Attractive?"

"Well, yeah, but candidly, he does nothing for my stomach."

"I don't care," said Gina. "If he doesn't come over here in about two seconds, I'm going over there."

The two seconds passed. Gina absently put her drink onto the bar and started a processional arc around the dance floor.

"Good luck," Alice called, then muttered to herself, "who would ever believe it."

Gina never once released the man's eye or wondered what she would say. A slow song played and several men tried to waylay her for a dance, but she brushed off each of them.

"We're staring," she said when she reached him. "Why?"

"Because we both know we don't belong here."

The man extended his hand toward the dance floor. It was crowded with couples grinding desperately to different music, but he and Gina danced perfectly. She looked deeply into his eyes,

then rested her head on his shoulder. His arms
made her feel warm, not with mere body heat but
with some form of communication she had never
felt before. She closed her eyes. She was spiral-
ing, ascending through clouds. Alice had told her
to meet people, and not to be surprised if something nice happened. Something had.

Out in the parking lot, Savage reflected on the
concept of the weeknight singles' dance. From
what he had observed, the title was a misnomer.
He could count at least a dozen cars rocking on
their springs, and most of these contained at least
one person he knew for a fact to be married. The
place was a divorce lawyer's dream.

Gina was the last person Savage expected to
see leave the club with her arm around a man.
The man was well over six feet tall and looked a
trim forty years old. The two walked to the far
end of the parking lot. Moments later, an engine
ignited and headlights cut the darkness.

Savage rolled his car through the lot. Once on
the highway, he realized he was following the
same dark-colored van that had stopped in front
of Gina's house. He doubted that this was a coincidence, but he didn't bother to speculate on
whether the man was her husband, an old friend,
or a pickup. Kate Lyons had disappeared on a
sunny afternoon while he sat on a bench with his
assumptions.

He followed the van into Greenhaven, an area
noted for large estates overlooking small inlets of
the Long Island Sound. It left the highway and

headed down an unlit private road. Savage kept his distance. He noticed several mansions with long driveways lined by trees and stone walls covered with ivy. The van continued downward, its taillights disappearing each time it took a curve. The air became cool and misty, with a hint of salt. Finally the van turned up a driveway toward a large mansion hidden behind a screen of evergreens. Savage ditched his car along a waist-high stone wall covered with branches of wildly overgrown shrubbery. He pulled himself over and struck out toward the mansion. Thorns nipped at his leisure suit, and his ankles wobbled over empty liquor bottles. Eventually he broke out near a circular drive. The evergreens fronting the mansion looked black in the mist. Savage took a deep breath, then sprinted to the trees. Dim lights burned in the windows. The van was nowhere in sight.

He reached the wall of the mansion without setting off any alarms, summoning any killer dogs, or tripping searchlights. He hoisted himself up to one of the windows. A library—empty. He let himself down, hurried across the stone entrance, and pulled himself up to another window. A fancy living room—empty, too.

Savage dropped to the ground and stroked his jowls. Maybe the man did not live in the mansion. The van could easily have rounded the circle and made it back to the highway while he was screwing around in the bushes. Then he noticed a gate and a dirt road running off the circle. The latch was padlocked, but the gate was wide enough for a van. He crouched and shined a pen-light on the ground. There were fresh tire tracks.

It took effort and an inch of seam from his pants, but Savage scaled the fence. The road curved into the darkness. Savage moved slowly and quietly, his eyes darting about for any sign of light or movement, his ears listening for any sound beyond his own breathing. The road descended and kept close to the mansion's wall. The tier of first floor windows receded higher and higher with every step. The basement windows were dark.

Dolingen parked the van in the garage behind the mansion. As she headed up the service road, she heard a clink of metal. She moved deep into the shadows and saw a fat man tottering on the gate. The man dropped heavily onto the road, then started to walk around the mansion, paying close attention to the windows. He was too big to be Ralph Lo Biasi, and whoever he was he must have followed them to the mansion. Calling the police was out of the question. It was the wrong time to have people swarming all over the grounds. And from the way this man was moving, he sensed something strange.

Dolingen stayed in the shadows until the man passed out of sight. Then she ran up the service road, stopping only to unlock the gate and swing it open.

* * *

As Savage neared the rear of the mansion he became aware of a humming sound like the idling of a car engine. He walked on and eventually found the road ended at a garage. The door was locked, but Savage could see the van through the window. He scratched his head. They had to be around here somewhere. The humming sound was now coming from behind him. He turned back toward the mansion.

Savage poked through the shrubbery covering the foundation, until he found a basement window. The glass was painted black, but small flecks of light leaked around the edges. Savage put his ear to the glass. The humming was louder. He scrambled to another window and found a spot where a paint bubble had burst. He planted his eye at the tiny hole.

He saw a basement workshop. In the center was a table, and on the table was a silver-and-glass cylinder that looked like a giant humidor. The cylinder was opened lengthwise and Gina, now dressed in a bodysuit, sat in the silver half. The man stood over her with his hands on her shoulders. She struggled weakly, as if drugged. He forced her to lie down then took out something resembling a vaccination gun and shot her in the left shoulder. Gina flopped around like a fish on the bottom of a boat. When she stopped, the man arranged her neatly, then closed the glass cover over her.

Savage pushed himself away from the window and wondered if he were dreaming or had just witnessed a ritual murder. He wished he could take a picture because there was no way in hell that anyone would believe this story. He stuck his eye back at the hole. The man lifted the cylinder onto his shoulder. A dozen more cylinders leaned against the back wall. Each contained a woman in a silver bodysuit.

Savage fought his way out of the shrubs and started up the dark roadway. The hell with Borley, he had to call the cops. This guy had either killed Gina or done something too weird to understand, and it looked like he had done it to a whole lot of other women, too. He would go to the cops right now, tell them what he saw, and make them swear out a search warrant.

Savage heard the tires screech just before the headlights came on. He never had a chance. The woman's face on the other side of the windshield grinned and his last thought was that the car was his own.

Chapter Twenty-three

———◆———

THE NEXT MORNING Dolingen took inventory of the cylinders stacked in the basement. Ninety-seven of the one hundred fifty cylinders Garno had brought were now occupied. Only four days remained in his allotted time. Much work lay ahead of them.

As Dolingen counted, Garno entered the room carrying a silver canister packed in dry ice. He gently set the canister down on the table and rubbed his hands in the vapor that billowed in the damp air. On the far end of the table was a battered wallet. He picked it up just as Dolingen turned from her work.

"We had an intruder last night," she said. "I found him on the service road just after I parked the van in the garage. He must have followed us here."

Garno emptied the contents of the wallet onto the table. There were several scraps of paper with scribbled writings, currency, and business cards.

"Why would this man follow us here?"

"He was a private investigator," said Dolingen. "Gina Lo Biasi, one of the children we retrieved last night, had a troubled marriage. After her sterility was discovered, her husband moved out of their house. I am certain he sent the investigator to gather evidence for a divorce proceeding."

"Where is this investigator now?" said Garno.

"I took care of him."

Garno shook his head. "The children are disconnected, but this man may not be. What about her husband? Will he not be concerned that his wife and the investigator are missing?"

"The man was right out there." Dolingen pointed up at the windows. Pinpoints of sunlight glistened in the black paint. "I could not be certain of what he had or had not seen. It was a calculated risk, but I can assure you that Gina's husband will be happy enough to be rid of his wife."

"I assume you have disposed of him," said Garno.

"And the vehicle. There is no possibility of discovery."

Garno stuffed the contents back into the wallet and tossed it onto the table. He walked slowly to an alcove formed by stacks of empty cylinders, his boot heels scraping on the concrete floor. He stared at the cylinders for a long time then swung his gaze to the frozen canister.

"How many remain?"

"Fifty-three," said Dolingen.

"If we are to continue to operate here, we must be extremely careful. No investigators, no close friends, no distraught lovers. I would rather lose one of our own than risk detection. Do any of the remaining fifty-three pose such a problem?"

Dolingen closed her eyes. The names of the children spun before her. Only one mattered.

"Her name is Nicole Bourne." Dolingen opened her eyes. "When she was very young, an old man who had made a fortune building ships befriended her. He has become so important in her life that she will not make a major decision without consulting him."

Garno sneered. "How could you allow such a bond to form?"

"There was so much to do with the relocation of the children, I could not concern myself with every prospective relationship. Besides, the man was already old. I did not think that he would be alive by your return. He has been unwittingly cooperative. Had Nicole not followed his advice, she would be well out of our reach, pursuing her career in places like California or Washington."

"Is her will that strong?"

"I am afraid so," said Dolingen.

"It is fortunate the man was helpful, but that is the past. I am concerned about them." Garno pointed at the canister. "A man of means in this society has the power to institute a search that could uncover our work. The risk is unacceptable."

Chapter Twenty-four

GARNO PICKED THROUGH the leafy shrubs until he could see into the window. The man called Hugh Michael Elliott was seated in an armchair, his eyes aimed at a pencil moving across a yellow pad on his lap. His thin white hair was neatly combed except for a swirl of muss where his hand scratched the back of his head.

Elliott tore the sheet from the pad, crumpled it, and tossed it over his shoulder. Several other discarded pages, wadded into balls, lay on the floor surrounding the armchair. Elliott resumed writing. After a minute of furious movement, he held up his pad and frowned.

A huge black woman entered the room and

placed a tea tray on the coffee table in front of the couch. Elliott put aside the pad and moved over from his armchair, furtively kicking the paper balls from sight. He sat on the couch, but when the woman started to pour the tea he waved her away.

"I'll take care of myself, Cassie. You can go up to bed if you'd like."

"Are you gonna be up all night again?" said the woman.

"Maybe. Building ships was easier than this."

"I'll be going up to bed, then," she said. "Don't leave so much paper under the chair this time."

Elliott laughed.

Garno backed out of the shrubs and walked around to the front porch. Through thick glass lights, he could see the blurry shape of the woman trudging up a staircase. The door was locked. He placed his finger on the cylinder and made a sharp circular motion. The latch slid back and he opened the door.

He went through an unlit dining room, taking each step carefully to prevent his boots from squeaking on the polished wood. He stopped at the sunroom doorway. Elliott now sat in a chair facing the far wall. His head bobbed and his hand scratched the pencil across the pad.

Garno drew a surge of power from his spine and concentrated on the line where Elliott's white hair ended and the shriveled skin of his neck began. Elliott's head held still, the pencil ceased to move. Garno stepped forward, the power pulsing in his arm, moving closer to his outstretched fingers.

Suddenly Elliott turned. He regarded Garno without surprise or fear.

"I thought I heard someone," he said.

"Yes." Garno let the power settle. He wanted to take a closer look at the man who had cast such a powerful influence over Nicole.

"Cassie didn't announce you." A troubled expression briefly crossed High's face.

"She did not see me."

"Yes. Well, I'm glad you're here, Rory. We have so much to discuss."

Rory. The name meant nothing to Garno. He could detect a fine mind and a strong will in Hugh Michael Elliott. But in the presence of the power, the old man's faculties were confused.

"For the last few days I've been trying to write about Nicole." Hugh lurched out of his chair. "I understand you are a poet, so you can appreciate that."

"I suppose I can."

"I thought I understood her perfectly until I started to write about her." Hugh knelt on the floor. With a sweep of his long arm he pulled the paper balls out from under the chair. "You can see I've had quite a few false starts."

Garno loomed over the old man. Hugh struggled to his feet, moving out of range. Garno's hand twitched.

"Now I know that you are interested in Nicole." Hugh's brow hardened. "I hope you aren't expecting me to act as a John Alden."

"No, I do not."

"It's nothing personal, mind you. I've just

made it a practice to stay out of Nicole's affairs of the heart."

"Very sensible," said Garno. He reached across the space between them, releasing his power the instant his fingers touched Hugh's chest. The old man went stiff. His eyes rolled back, his tongue clucked against the roof of his mouth. Garno withdrew his hand and Hugh collapsed onto the chair.

"Very sensible indeed."

Garno straightened the body, crossed one leg over the other, and put the yellow pad on his lap. He worked a pencil into the long fingers. Then he kicked all the paper balls under the chair so that no one could say that Hugh Michael Elliott was not neat until the end.

Chapter Twenty-five

———◆———

NICOLE POUNDED THE top of her digital alarm-clock, but the ringing did not stop. She unstuck her eyelids; it was 6:12. The day's schedule passed before her: two job interviews that were good prospects and a dinner date with Rory that could turn ugly. Still, it seemed awfully early to have the alarm set. Then she realized the ringing was the telephone.

Her hand found the receiver and pulled it to her ear. At first she heard no one at the other end. She was about to say something nasty when she heard a whimper. The whimper resolved into words.

"Miz Nicole?"

Cassie. A dead weight fell through Nicole's stomach. She sat bolt upright.

"Miz Nicole. It's Mr. Hugh."

"What about Hugh?"

The whimper started again.

"Cassie, what's wrong with Hugh?"

"He's—"

"Tell me."

"He's dead."

"What?" said Nicole, even though she had heard.

"I gave him his tea at eleven. He said he'd be up late and I should go on to bed. He didn't need me. When I came down this morning the sunroom light was on. He was just sitting there. He didn't move."

"Cassie, are you sure he's dead. Are you sure he's not—" But she did not know what.

"I'm sure. The police, ambulance, they all were here."

"I'm coming over right now."

She hung up and buried her face in the pillows. Hugh leaped into view, playing on the back of her eyelids. It was last Saturday and he was posing ridiculously like Charles Atlas in his Chinese robe.

"You'll be happy to know that the doctor said I just might live forever."

Nicole choked on something between a laugh and a sob. She pushed herself out of bed and stumbled to the dresser. Tears welled up in her eyes as she stuffed dark-colored clothes into an overnight bag.

Nicole took a taxi because she could not trust herself to drive. Cassie was waiting in the open doorway of Hugh's house. Her face was swollen from crying. They embraced, Cassie's strong arms digging into the small of Nicole's back.

"What happened?" Nicole said when they broke away.

Cassie turned in the direction of the sunroom, her usual waddle now more of a shuffle.

"He wanted to write. All he talked about for the last week was his writing. Then yesterday afternoon he tells me, 'Cassie, I'm gonna do it.' 'Do what,' I says. 'Write,' he says and runs around like a chicken without a head. I was cooking a roast beef. He didn't want it. Made me fix him lentil soup and a salad. I don't know why. Then he doesn't want to be disturbed, 'cept for tea at eleven o'clock. That was the last time I saw him. Wouldn't let me pour the tea for him. Said he was a big boy."

They stood in the sunroom. Nicole noticed a line of sharpened pencils and a pile of yellow pads on the coffee table. The cushions of his favorite armchair sagged. Another yellow pad lay on the brandy table next to the armchair. There was writing on the first page.

"Would you like anything, Miz Nicole?"

"No, Cassie, thank you. I'd just like to stay here for a few minutes."

Nicole waited until she heard Cassie's battered slippers shuffling across the wood of the dining room floor before she reached for the yellow pad. The handwriting was sloppy, as if his thoughts had come in waves and he could change only a few into words as they broke over him. But Nicole was accustomed to his handwriting and could make sense out of the scribble.

It began with footprints in the dew.

Nicole pulled the paper from the pad and folded it. A tear welled out of her eye, followed by another and another. There was no reason to unravel any more of Hugh's words. She knew how the story ended.

Chapter Twenty-six

———◆———

BORLEY AWOKE WITH his head on the computer table in Karen's old study. His mouth tasted like gunmetal. His left arm was numb. Inches away were a tape recorder, the tapes of his sessions with Nicole, the photographs of Valerie and the nurse, and two empty beer cans. Everything shone.

Once Borley realized the brightness was from

sunlight in the windows, he pushed himself up
with his good arm and reached for the phone.
Savage's voice repeated the message from the
night before. Nothing else was on the office answering machine, not even a hang-up. He scribbled "Shore Club" on a note pad, then called
Savage's apartment. He hung up after the third
ring. Even Savage should have answered by then.

As Borley drove to Savage's apartment he explained the telephone silence to himself. Nothing
interesting had happened at the Shore Club and
Savage was at home with the phone unplugged
so that he could sleep. It made perfect sense, except he knew he was kidding himself.

Savage's Plymouth was nowhere around his
house. The window shades were pulled tight.
Borley rang the bell three times, pounded the
door twice, and finished with a kick. Savage was
not home.

The next stop was Gina's. A *New York Times*
wrapped in blue plastic lay at the foot of her
driveway, but he had seen that before. He cut the
engine and walked up to the garage. A beat-up
Oldsmobile was inside, but Savage had reported
Gina was with her friend. Once again, he knew he
was kidding himself.

He went up a set of flagstone steps wedged into
the side of a hill. The backyard lawn and shrubbery were overgrown, as if each Lo Biasi wanted
the place to go to hell to spite the other. He remembered the gazebo from Gina's story about
the night of the meteor, the night her childhood
fantasy had returned. He rang a metal bell attached to the back door. No one responded. He

moved from window to window. Several kitchen cabinets were open, showing nothing inside. Ralph was beginning to pick the place clean. Newspapers were stacked on the dining room table. A plate lay face down on the floor. Borley tried the front bell just for the hell of it but did not wait for an answer.

Borley found the Shore Club with no trouble. The parking lot was littered with crushed plastic cups, dirty napkins, and tattered paper leis. One car was parked near the entrance. It was not Savage's.

The front door was open and a man's voice sang along with country music from a tinny AM radio. Chairs were upended on tables, paper bunting hung limply from the ceiling, a fake palm lay on its side. The man pushed a heap of wet paper with a mop.

"Hello," said Borley.

The man stopped mopping. Borley walked across the sticky floor.

"I'm looking for two people. A fella by the name of Savage and a woman named Gina Lo Biasi."

"Nobody here but me," said the man. "Last people cleared out around four."

"I know they were here at nine."

"Them and three hundred other people." The man poked his mop at the pile. "What do they look like?"

"Savage is about my height, but he has a big gut, a walrus mustache, and a bald spot. Gina's thirty-ish. Thin with pale skin and dark hair."

"If they were here, I didn't notice them."

"What about her?" Borley took the photo of the nurse from his pocket.

The man looked carefully at the picture. "I didn't notice her, either."

"What went on here last night?" said Borley.

"Singles' dance," said the man. "Pretty good crowd, too. You should try it sometime. Guy with your looks can do pretty well here. Especially with the young chicks."

"Maybe I will," said Borley.

"Another one next week," said the man. "It's wild. Anything can happen."

"Yeah," said Borley. He turned toward the door. Once again, anything had happened.

Borley tried Savage and Gina every hour from his office. By mid-afternoon he gave up. He paced behind his desk, stopping occasionally to rearrange the tapes or to reread the old newspaper articles but mostly to look at the photograph of the nurse.

He walked across the corridor to the window. Small clouds hurried past the sun, causing the parking lot to dim and brighten in quick succession. He wondered whether he should tell Nicole the real nature of his study. As late as yesterday he could not imagine himself explaining brain chemicals, stimuli, and women who acted like sick cats, as Savage had put it that night in his apartment. It seemed fantastic, even though thirty years' work had uncovered no more plausible explanation. The last few hours proved one thing: Savage's theory was winning.

At precisely four o'clock, the telephone rang. It was Nicole.

"Borley, I'm afraid I must cancel our dinner plans."

"Problem?"

"A big one," said Nicole. "Hugh passed away last night."

"I'm sorry to hear that."

"I'll be staying at his house for a day or so to make the funeral arrangements. I'm the only one who can do it. He outlived his family and close friends."

"Was it expected?"

"As much as it can be for a man in his eighties. He just had a complete physical last week." Nicole forced a laugh. "The doctor told him he might live forever."

There was a brief silence. Borley thought she might have the phone covered with her hand.

"Are you all right?" he said.

"Under the circumstances."

"Is everything else all right?"

"I'm not sure what you mean."

Neither did Borley.

"Nothing," he said. "So you'll be staying at Hugh's house in Milton."

"I don't feel much like partying," said Nicole. She sounded tired.

"Call if you need anything," said Borley. "Even if it's just to talk."

"Sure, Borley. Thanks."

Borley stared at the telephone. Before he could formulate his next move, it rang again. It was the student who had wanted an appointment to discuss his final grade. Borley said he would be unavailable until classes resumed.

Chapter Twenty-seven

BORLEY SPREAD A 1:100,000 map of the area on his desk and took the phone book down from the shelf. There were listings for hospitals, clinics, medical centers, professional buildings, nursing homes, and sanitariums. Hospitals seemed to be the most logical choice. He counted fifteen within a ten-mile radius of his office.

Borley ripped the pages out of the phone book and ran to his car. The administrative nurse at the first hospital refused to give out any information about anyone on her staff. Period. She did not care who he was or how important it might be to find the nurse in the photograph. Borley left with the distinct impression that she suspected he was a rapist. The administrative nurse at the second hospital was not as stern. She would have liked to help him but, really, she needed to see some credentials. Borley had none. She was terribly sorry. The head nurse at the third hospital took a different tack. Instead of invoking her authority, she looked carefully at the photograph and announced she had never seen the nurse. In fact, during her twenty-odd years in hospital administration, she had never seen a nurse who even faintly resembled the woman in the photograph.

Borley thanked her profusely for narrowing his search and walked out into the warm twilight. His approach was all wrong. Savage would have come out with something more than the address of the next hospital on the list. If only he could call him. But Savage was gone, along with Kate, Gina, Valerie, Sarah Grover, Mary Ann Fitzgerald, and the hundreds of other women whose names he had uncovered over the years.

At the fourth hospital, St. Catherine's, two nurses stood behind the reception desk in the lobby. One was forty-ish with pretty features thickened by too many night-shift snacks. The other seemed barely out of her teens. Several people were lined up for visitors' passes. Borley waited for a lull.

"Hello, who are you here to see?" said the younger nurse. The name on her identification plate was Moira Fitzryan.

"No one," said Borley. He removed the photo from his pocket and placed it face down on the counter. "I'm trying to locate someone, a nurse."

"What's her name?" The older nurse elbowed herself between them.

"That I don't know. All I have is this." Borley turned over the photograph. Both nurses looked, but only the older one spoke.

"She's not on the staff here, I can tell you that. She does look familiar, though. I might have seen her around. Maybe she's a per diem."

"What's that?" said Borley.

"An agency nurse," said Moira. "They have no steady assignment. An agency sends them on a day to day basis wherever they are needed."

"So this woman might be working anywhere," said Borley.

"Right," said the older one. "At a hospital, a clinic, even somebody's home."

Borley tapped his fingers on the counter.

"Any way of finding the agency?" he said.

"Not without her name," said the older nurse.

"What if I told you her name might be Dolly?"

"A 'might be' first name wouldn't help."

Borley thanked them and put the photograph back into his pocket. Across the lobby was a bank of vending machines. He plunked in fifty cents for a cup of coffee, hoping he got something approximating cream and sugar. As usual, it tasted like hot water. As he turned to dump it into the refuse can, he noticed Moira beside him.

"You can't be this desperate for coffee," he said.

"Meet me outside," she said as she fed coins into the machine.

Borley left the lobby and stood on the sidewalk around the corner from the entrance. A minute later Moira came from the other direction.

"I couldn't tell you in front of her." Moira nodded toward the lobby doors. "Your nurse has been here."

"When?"

"Several times. The latest was the other night,

I think." Moira looked around quickly. She seemed troubled.

"What happened?"

"I was on the night shift, checking rooms on the fifth floor. There was an accident patient named Elizabeth Donahue. She was in a coma and all I had to do was record the readings on the monitors. When I walked into the room, your nurse was standing there. I asked who she was and what she was doing. She told me she was a private-duty nurse and to mind my own business. It seemed strange. I was going to call the head nurse, but something touched me behind the ear and the next thing I knew I was on the toilet."

"Sounds like a dream."

"It wasn't," Moira insisted. "I definitely walked into that room and definitely spoke to your woman. Then I was on the toilet. I don't remember anything in between."

"Did you report this?"

"No."

"Why not?"

"Because," said Moira, "when I walked out of the bathroom, Elizabeth Donahue was dead."

"Then I need to know some things about her," said Borley.

They went through the emergency room, down a short corridor marked HOSPITAL STAFF ONLY, and entered a small room containing computer equipment. Moira pulled a diskette from a tightly packed mechanical filing cabinet and seated herself at the terminal.

"I've been teaching myself computers," she said.

"You can never know too much," said Borley.

Moira inserted the diskette in the disk drive and punched the keyboard. The screen filled with information about Elizabeth Donahue.

"I'm mostly interested in her age and place of birth," said Borley.

Moira scrolled down the file. Elizabeth Donahue was twenty-nine and had been born in Syracuse. She was admitted with severe internal and head injuries on July 29, 1985. She had been on life-support for her entire stay. The immediate cause of death was myocardial infarction.

"Exactly why didn't you report that nurse?" said Borley.

"I guess because I didn't understand what happened with me waking up on the toilet."

"But this death has upset you."

Moira nodded. "She was in a bad way, but I never expected she would die so soon."

"Is there anything you know about Elizabeth that doesn't appear in the file?"

"I heard something about her parents fixing a room in their house so they could take her home. Then she had a seizure and the doctors wouldn't allow it."

Borley stroked his chin.

"Why are you looking for this nurse?" said Moira.

"I'm not sure," he said. "But I didn't think it was murder."

Borley showed Moira the list of hospitals he planned to visit, and she marked the three that used the most per diem nurses. She also promised to call Borley if she saw the nurse again. The first two hospitals proved fruitless, but at the third, Florence Hospital, he found a security guard who recognized the woman in the photograph. The guard was pretty sure she was working the night shift. Borley asked permission to look around for her. The guard wanted to see some credentials. Borley pulled out a twenty and the guard waved him past.

"If you get caught, I don't know you," he said.

Borley winked. Savage would have been proud.

The corridors were empty. He ducked into a room marked LAUNDRY and donned a set of soiled whites he found in a canvas basket, feeling like a character in a farcical detective movie. The shirt hung from his shoulders like a sack. The pants bagged around his ankles to cover his jeans. His sneakers squeaked on the linoleum.

Out in the corridor, voices rose and two nurses rounded a corner. Borley focused on infinity to look preoccupied, then at the last minute nodded in greeting. The nurses responded with hellos.

Borley covered three of the five hospitals floors without finding anyone who resembled his nurse. He took the fire stairs to the fourth floor and caught a glimpse of a tall figure disappearing into a room at the end of the corridor. He followed, walking slowly on the sides of his feet so that his sneakers would not squeak.

She came out before he reached the room. She looked exactly as he had expected—black hair worn in a single thick braid, vaguely Oriental eyes, thin mouth—but in person there was a strange detachment missing from Valerie's drawing and Savage's photograph. Something heavy swung in the pocket of her smock. She steadied it with her forearm and passed Borley without meeting his eye. He turned into the first doorway and watched her until she made a right turn at the end of the corridor. Then he entered the room she had just left. A woman of about fifty lay on the window bed. She snorted and rolled over from one side to the other. On the other bed a woman in her twenties slept on her back with her knees raised. The corners of her mouth were turned up in a faint smile.

Borley covered the rest of the floor in double time, sneaking glances into every room. The nurse was nowhere to be seen. He took the stairs up to the fifth floor and was about to push through the fire door when he noticed her enter the room directly across the corridor. He kept his eyes at the window.

The nurse approached the bed on the far side of the room. She looked at the chart, then pulled the sheet down to expose the legs of a woman. She gently raised each knee, then spread the legs apart. She uncoiled a long rubber tube from the pocket holding the heavy object and placed its end in the woman's vagina. The woman's legs wobbled.

A hand clapped onto Borely's shoulder and pulled him away from the window. Borley spun, his face scraping across the brass buttons of a blue uniform shirt, then his back smashed against the cinderblock wall. A big black security guard grinned down at him.

"What the hell is going on here?" said the guard.

"That's what I'm trying to find out," said Borley. He pushed himself off the wall. "That nurse—"

The guard slammed him back.

"What about the nurse?"

"She's doing something to the woman in the room across the hall."

The guard grabbed a handful of Borley's shirt and moved so that he could peer through the window.

"I don't see no nurse."

"She's right across the hall."

The guard gave Borley a long, disgusted look, then shoved him up against the window. The nurse was no longer in the room. The woman on the bed lay still with the sheet covering her raised legs.

"Let's go."

The guard pushed Borley through the door and dragged him around to the elevator. Borley turned his head wildly but did not see the nurse anywhere. The guard kept his grip on Borley's shirt during the entire ride down to the ground floor.

The security office had a large one-way glass window facing the lobby. Behind the desk sat the guard who had let Borley in for the twenty. He made good on his promise to forget they had ever met.

"Should I search him, Captain?"

"Nah." The captain came out from behind the desk and looked Borley from head to toe. "What the hell are you doing sneaking around this hospital after midnight?"

"I'm writing a book about health care," said Borley. "This is research."

"He said something about a nurse," said the guard.

"A nurse?" said the captain. He took Borley's twenty from his shirt pocket and folded it several times. "We have plenty of those. Florence Hospital has the best nurses around. What about this nurse?"

"He said she was doing something to a woman patient," said the guard.

"Did you investigate?"

"Yeah. I didn't see nothing."

The captain turned his attention to Borley. "So why the whites?"

"I was trying to avoid the Heisenberg Uncertainty Principle."

"Sounds like a wiseass to me," said the guard.

"Get 'em off," said the captain.

Borley let the huge pants drop around his feet. As he worked out of the shirt, he noticed a figure moving through the lobby. The nurse was leaving.

"Get the fuck out of here," said the captain. "If I see you again it'll be the police."

Borley moved toward the door, but the guard blocked his path.

"Is that the way you leave your clothes?"

Borley gathered the whites into a bundle and

dropped them on the desk. Then he ran out the door.

"Forget him," said the captain. He unfolded the twenty. "Let's send for a pizza."

Borley searched the entire parking lot but did not find the nurse.

Chapter Twenty-eight

————◆————

THE LOCAL NEWSPAPER gave the Hugh Michael Elliott obituary an eleven-point headline and four inches of copy. Elliott was born in Hartford, Connecticut, in 1905. After attending Oxford and graduating from Harvard, he served in the United States Navy, attaining the rank of ensign. In 1932, he founded H. M. Enterprises, a shipbuilding company on City Island, New York. During his long career he helped design three America's Cup winners. His only marriage ended in divorce when he was twenty-six. He left no survivors.

Borley folded the newspaper and tossed it onto the passenger seat. One block away, a man wearing a green custodian outfit swept the walkway leading to the front steps of the Church of Christ. Borley checked his watch; the funeral cortege was already late.

The custodian shouldered his broom and disappeared around the side of the church. At the
same moment, Borley noticed a set of headlights
in his rearview mirror. He slouched down in his
seat as a dark-gray hearse moved slowly past.
The hearse parked directly in front of the walkway, and the rest of the funeral party settled in
behind. Borley counted eight cars, including the
hearse and a limousine. Hugh Michael Elliott had
outlived a good number of people.

Only Nicole and a heavyset black woman Borley assumed was Cassie emerged from the limousine. They stood motionless as the pallbearers
slid the coffin out of the rear of the hearse and
hoisted it onto their shoulders. When the coffin
passed, Cassie hooked her thick arm around Nicole's elbow and they went into the church.

The service was short. Afterward, Borley followed the funeral through the center of Milton
and into Greenlawn Cemetery on the other side of
town. He parked just inside the gate and watched
the other cars wind up the slope through the
ranks of headstones that were bright white in the
sun. The hearse stopped near a small mausoleum
at the top of the hill and a man in a black suit
signaled the limousine and the other cars to tuck
in close behind. Borley watched from a distance
until the minister closed his prayer book and the
mourners moved slowly forward to toss flowers
on the crypt. Soon only Cassie and Nicole were
left. Cassie threw her flower, then reached up to
touch Nicole's shoulder. Nicole seemed not to notice. Cassie broke into sobs and waddled away.
Finally, Nicole let the flower drop from her hand,

but instead of returning to the cars she walked beyond the mausoleum. She stood in the short, noontime shadow of an obelisk and pulled her dark suit jacket about her as if she felt a sudden chill.

Borley moved closer. Car doors slammed shut and engines fired back to life, but Nicole did not move. He drew up beside her.

"I'm sorry."

She nodded and a tear hurried down her cheek.

"I always thought crying at a funeral was glib, that people were really crying for themselves. Now I'm not so sure."

Borley noticed Cassie approaching at the edge of his vision. She motioned for him to get Nicole's attention, but he waved her away.

"I've walked around his house in a trance the past couple of days," Nicole said to her hands. "I slept on the sofa in the sunroom where Cassie found him and wished I would see a ghost, hear a voice, anything to make me believe he could walk back into my life when I needed him. We take people for granted when they're alive, and I'm just as guilty of that as anyone."

Borley noticed Cassie walking back toward the open door of the limousine. The door closed and the engine started.

"But I never took Hugh for granted. Oh, I didn't see as much of him as either of us would have wanted. But he understood."

Nicole looked from her hands to the sky. A jet moved across at a great altitude, leaving a thin white contrail behind.

"The sky's really blue today."

"The humidity will be back," said Borley. "It's still August."

Nicole looked past the mausoleum. "Oh no, everyone's gone."

"Don't worry. I can give you a lift."

Chapter Twenty-nine

———◆———

NICOLE DIRECTED BORLEY to the large ivy-covered house now owned by the estate of Hugh Michael Elliott. He parked in the driveway behind a gardener's truck dusted with dried grass clippings. At the farthest end of the great lawn, the gardener rode a power mower hard against the curve of the stone wall.

"Twentieth century bogeyman," said Nicole.

Borley noted the evergreen shrubs dotting the grass. Even now, twenty years after Hugh had leaped out to capture Nicole, they looked hardly large enough to hide a man.

"So this is where it all started," he said.

"My second birth," Nicole said, forcing joy into the words. "Let's go inside."

Nicole showed him the great hall, where she had spent the first hours of her second birth, and the sunroom, where Hugh had spent the last hours of his life. She brought him upstairs to a guest room. The bed was white cane and the dresser was white lacquer. There was a mahogany desk in one corner and above it shelves filled with law books.

"Hugh bought it all for me," said Nicole. "I never was able to concentrate at home so I studied here until I could afford my own apartment."

As Nicole gathered her clothes from the bed, Borley walked over to the open window. He could hear the hum of the mower and smell the cut grass. It was a safe place, a cozy scene—a determined young woman studying in the mansion of her elderly mentor. He wondered if Valerie had felt as secure in the room she had used as her studio.

"I need one more thing," said Nicole.

She led him up a stairway lined with walls of crumbling plaster. The attic was stifling. A wasp floated by, its wings buzzing in the thick air. They shouldered past dusty wardrobes, pyramids of books covered with clear plastic, and wounded outdoor statuary she described as her introduction to sculpture. She opened a door to a small room created from a dormer. Inside were several cardboard boxes, and atop one sat an antique sextant. She cradled the sextant in her arms.

"Hugh taught me how to use this when I was in sixth grade," she said. "I don't care what his will says. This is mine. Never can tell when I'll need to navigate by the stars."

Outside, Borley stowed Nicole's overnight bag in the Starion's trunk. He slammed down the lid and found her staring at him.

"Do you have any plans?" she said.

"No."

"I'm not ready to face my apartment just yet. We could have that dinner we missed."

"Do you have a particular place in mind?"

"I leave it to you," said Nicole. "I can't make any decisions at the moment."

Borley drove north on Interstate 684. The air conditioner blasted against the heat of the wide sky, but he felt sweat on his neck and noticed Nicole rustling uncomfortably in her black suit. He exited the highway and took shady back roads to his house.

"Have I just been kidnapped?" Nicole said as he turned into the cul de sac.

"Not exactly." said Borley. He showed her the downstairs bathroom, then waited in the backyard while she traded her suit for something from her overnight bag. Sunlight radiated off the burnt grass. August insects chattered in the trees. Borley dragged two lawn chairs into the small area of shade created by the house. Once again he wondered how anything bad could happen literally in his own backyard. Then he remembered the yogurt shop, the three hundred singles at the Shore Club, and himself sitting on the front porch of the farmhouse as a night that had lasted thirty years descended. He could not be too careful.

The screen door banged. Borley saw that the something from Nicole's overnight bag had turned out to be cutoff jeans and a black T-shirt. She bounced down the steps, barefoot.

"Would you like a drink?" said Borley.

"Gin or vodka," said Nicole.

Borley went into the kitchen and made two gin-and-tonics. He returned to find Nicole lounging on one of the lawn chairs. He pulled the other close.

"It must be nice to sit out here at night," she said after taking a sip. She lay back and lifted her head. "The sky always seemed more interesting when I lived upstate."

"Less light pollution," said Borley.

"That's true," said Nicole. "But I think my eyes have become jaded. I remember looking out my window when I was supposed to be asleep and seeing satellites cross the sky. How many children do that today?"

"No idea."

"There was the fireball the other night. That was interesting. Did you see it?"

"I couldn't avoid it."

"You make it sound like something negative. Someone once told me that seeing a shooting star means you will fall in love." Nicole smirked. "Funny, things didn't work out with him."

"Where were you when the fireball fell?"

"At my apartment window, just like the little girl who watched for satellites. What about you?"

"I was in a field."

"Doing what?"

"Believe it or not, we were there to watch the meteor shower."

"So you weren't alone."

"No, but the fireball made me realize I wasn't in love." Borley took a sip and let the words settle.

"Maybe the two people shouldn't be together when they see the shooting star," said Nicole.

"Maybe."

"Borley." Nicole swung her legs off the lounge. "I'm not very good at innuendo. The most important person in my life has just made the grand exit. The past two days have been a kaleidoscope of grief, insecurity, and loneliness. I found myself thinking about you a lot."

"And I've been thinking about you."

"Hugh always said that I did things for more than one reason. He called it my psychological insurance policy. I answered your ad because I was bothered by something I couldn't discuss with anyone. Not even Hugh. The moment I walked into your office, I knew this could happen. And if it didn't, we still had our conversations."

Borley brushed her cheek with his fingers and gently guided her lips to his.

"I've wanted to do that for a long time," she said when they parted.

"Not as long as I have," said Borley.

He took her hand and led her across the dry grass to the shed. The air inside was cool and smelled faintly of dry wood. He kissed her hard on the mouth. She worked at his belt. He slipped the T-shirt over her head and felt her nipples rise against his chest. Then he eased her onto the daybed.

Chapter Thirty

———◆———

BORLEY AWOKE ON the inside half of the bed and
untangled himself from Nicole's legs. She mumbled weakly and fell back to sleep, her panties
dropping from her ankle to the floor. He went to
the doorway. The sun was still well up in the sky
and the burnt grass shimmered in the heat. He
turned back toward Nicole. The light cast her
body into low relief. She seemed to be running
with one leg bent at the knee and the other leg
straight.

Borley stepped into his jeans. He left the door
open a crack and ran up the back steps to the
kitchen. The cupboards held dry soup, canned
tuna, and an old jar of instant coffee that defied
gravity when turned upside down. The refrigerator contained nothing but a tub of crumby mar-
garine, a half-empty bottle of tonic, and a quart
of milk way past its expiration date. The freezer
had only ice cubes.

He hastily mixed two gin-and-tonics and returned to the shed. Nicole was no longer running,
but she was still asleep. He placed her drink on
the floor next to the bed and leaned against the
wall. For thirty years he had pursued his theory,
rejecting the assumptions of men like Savage as
cynical and treating the ramblings of women like
Mrs. Grover as absurd. Now he realized the explanation could be a combination of all three: the
chemical, the human, perhaps even the divine.
For the moment, however, the explanation was

irrelevant. He did not care about the nurse or her motives. All he cared about was keeping Nicole safe.

Borley watched her sleep until the drink grew warm in his hand. When she began to stir, he downed the gin and kissed her the moment she opened her eyes.

"Welcome back," he said.

"How long was I asleep?"

"Not very long. It's still summer out there, still afternoon for that matter." He handed her the gin and tonic.

Nicole sat up and took a healthy sip. Borley settled onto a sliver of the bed.

"You have an interesting toolshed, Borley," she said. "Do you always entertain like this?"

"No."

She reached over Borley and placed her drink on the floor.

"Just teasing," she said with a laugh. She climbed out of bed, playfully kissing him as she moved past, and crouched over the pile of bird prints. "What do you really use this shed for? Awh, I see. It's an art gallery."

"Right," said Borley.

"Nice." Nicole flipped through the prints. "Who did these?"

"A woman named Valerie Kennedy. You probably never heard of her. She's a relative unknown."

"She shouldn't be. These are so well drawn they could be photographs." Nicole noticed the easel with the covered canvas. She stood. "May I?"

Borley nodded. Nicole turned back the cover.

Her hand went to her mouth as if she saw something horrible. Then her expression softened. She moved closer, entranced, and slowly drew her fingers along the line of faceless couples, through the austere building, and out the other side, eventually settling on the shoulders of the two figures in the foreground.

"What is it called?"

"*American Gothic 2100 A.D.*"

"It's beautiful." She noticed the initials in the lower right corner of the canvas. "Same artist?"

"Yes."

"I never would expect the person who did those prints to paint this," said Nicole. "Did you know her?"

"Sort of." Borley rose from the bed and embraced Nicole from behind, each hand cupping a breast. Her eyes remained fixed on the canvas.

"Did she ever explain this painting?"

"Not to me." He nuzzled the back of her neck, trying to draw her away.

"It gives me an odd feeling."

Borley stiffened. "What kind?"

"Hard to explain. It's not quite a déjà vu. Nostalgia, maybe." She finally turned from the painting and nestled her face in his chest. "It's not important."

Borley stared at the faceless couple, tempted to warn her about what had happened to the artist and to another young woman whose dreams had resembled the painting. Instead, he squeezed her tightly.

"I thought we were having dinner," she said.

"We are, but we have a small problem. No food in the house."

"You were going to cook for me?"

"I still am. Do you like Szechuan chicken?"

"If made by a master."

"Then you'll love mine."

Nicole dressed and they went inside the house. Borley extracted an old, well-oiled wok from a cupboard filled with pots. Then he rummaged through a junk drawer until he found a creased photocopy of a recipe.

"And now to the store."

"Is it far from here?" said Nicole.

"About a ten minute drive. There are closer stores, but I'm out of my special spices."

"Why don't you run over while I take a bath. I feel gritty."

Borley bit his lip, calculating.

"Did I say something wrong?" she said.

"No," he said. "I would miss you for twenty minutes."

"Don't be silly." She gave him a kiss. "I'll make you glad you came back."

"All right. It's not that long a time," he said as much to himself as to her. "But do me a favor and keep the doors locked until I get back."

"Sure, Borley. Is this a bad neighborhood?"

"No, but it's quiet, and sometimes bad things happen."

"Such as?"

"Bad things." He sounded like someone's father, lecturing how he knew best. "Burglaries."

"Do you have a baseball bat I can take into the bath with me?" Nicole teased.

"I might."

"You're serious."

Borley looked out the window at the sunlight. It was still early.

"No, just a worrier," he said. He embraced her and she responded.

"I'll keep the door locked," she said.

Borley set her up with towels, shampoo, even liquid bubble-bath Karen had left behind. As Nicole drew her bath, he checked the back door latch and the front door deadbolt. Both seemed fine, as always. When he returned to the kitchen, he could hear Nicole splashing in the tub. He pushed open the door and saw her covered with bubbles and aiming the sextant at the ceiling.

"All I need are some boats to play with," she said.

Borely's face hardened.

"I'm only kidding."

He exaggerated a smile.

"Is everything all right, Borley?"

"Fine," he said. "I'll be going now."

"Hurry back," said Nicole. "This bath is reminding me how hungry I am."

Borley checked both doors from the outside before he fired up the Starion. He eased down to the foot of the cul de sac. Nothing seemed amiss, no suspicious cars, no strange people lurking behind bushes. He turned onto the highway and shot the Starion into overdrive, the turbocharger whistling. He slowed down only once, to let a light change at a crossroads where a girl was selling flowers out of the back of a truck. He decided he would stop on his way home. A bouquet would make up for his weird behavior.

He reached the market in record time and quickly filled a shopping basket with two bottles of white wine and the ingredients for Szechuan chicken. The checkout line was mercifully short. He paid with exact change.

One the way back, Borley relaxed. The highway was empty and he guided the Starion easily along the sweeping curves. He whistled with the turbocharger. Nicole was probably still in the tub. If he made it home in time he would join her. It would be a pleasant way to kill one bottle of wine.

Borley was less than halfway home when the Starion's engine suddenly cut out. He quickly pulled onto the shoulder. No dashboard lights flashed and all the instruments were in order. He floored the accelerator in neutral. The engine wheezed and the tachometer needle quivered weakly around five hundred RPMs. He released the hood latch and got out of the car. The engine shook on its mountings.

Borley went back behind the wheel and switched off the ignition. He waited a minute, then turned the key. The engine hummed smoothly. He gave it some gas; the tachometer jumped toward the red line. He started back onto the highway, carefully working through the gears until he made it to fifth. Whatever was wrong before, the car seemed fine now.

But it happened again. Borley was on the crest of a hill when the engine died. He shifted into neutral and let the Starion coast toward a gas station he could see half a mile away. The car had just enough momentum to make it. An attendant limped over, wringing a greasy red towel in his hands. He had big arms and a large birthmark on one cheek. "Charlie" was stitched over his shirt pocket.

"Car sounds sick," he said.

"It just cut out at the top of the hill," said Borley. "Watch."

He pressed the gas pedal and the engine sputtered.

"Pop the lid and let's have a look."

Borley released the lock and Charlie hoisted the hood.

"Looks like a goddam plate of spaghetti," said Charlie. He leaned his ear close to the engine.

"Do you have a phone I could use?" said Borley.

Chapter Thirty-one

———•———

NICOLE STAYED IN the tub for only a short time. The warm water, softened by the bubble bath, made her drowsy and she drifted back to Hugh, hearing his voice, feeling his shoulder bones when they embraced, smelling the faint aroma of pipe tobacco that pervaded his great hall even though he never smoked. She placed the sextant on the ledge behind her head and unplugged the stopper with her toe. She did not want to think of him at the moment. She would work through his death in her own time. Right now she was with Borley Share. Hugh would understand. He always had.

Nicole tucked a towel around herself and went out into the kitchen. The fresh air did not revive her, so she searched the cupboard for coffee. She found an old jar of instant that still smelled drinkable. A few knocks with the heel of her hand loosened enough for a cup. No kettle was in immediate sight, so she ran tap water into a quart pot and put it on the stove to boil.

The telephone rang. She followed the sound into a back room that looked like an office. There was a desk, an empty computer table, and two file cabinets. The phone, at the end of a long, tangled cord, was perched so precariously on the highest shelf of the computer table that the ringing threatened to topple it to the floor. Nicole gingerly lifted the receiver.

"Nicole, Borley." A sound like a jackhammer rose in the background.

"Oh, it's you. I wasn't sure if I should answer. Sometimes you learn terrible things."

"Like I have another woman? Forget it." Borley waited for the jackhammer to stop.

"What's that sound?"

"An air compressor. I'm having some car trouble. The goddam thing keeps cutting out on me."

"Where are you?" Nicole recognized tapes

lying on the desk that were from her sessions with Borley.

"At a gas station."

"That's a good start." Nicole settled into the desk chair as Borley started to defend the remaining virtues of Japanese sports-cars. A tiny pair of eyes stared at her from the shadow of the computer table's shelf. Nicole shuddered, then realized the eyes belonged to a photograph. Borley's voice fought with the jackhammer. Nicole reached into the shelf and drew the photograph into the light. The face was oddly familiar.

Borley's voice faded as Nicole rooted around with her hand. Other photographs and a crumpled note fell to the table top. The photos showed the same woman dressed in a nurse's uniform. The odd feeling lingered. She could not describe it, but she knew when she had felt it before: when she uncovered the painting in the toolshed. The note was addressed to Borley from someone named Karen. The words "Good luck with the new doll you have found for your dollhouse" leaped off the page. She looked again at the photograph.

"Borley," she said, but so low he did not hear it over his own voice. She let it drop; she did not know what else to say.

"I'm not sure when I'll be home," said Borley. "I locked the doors when I left. Keep them locked. Don't let anyone else in but me. Okay?"

"Okay."

"Are you all right?"

"Yes. Are you?"

"Just a little pissed off at the moment," said

Borley. "Look, I know it sounds strange. I know I might sound strange. But I'll explain everything to you when I get home."

"Fine," said Nicole.

"I'll be there as soon as I can."

"No problem. Just make sure your car is fixed."

Borley laughed and hung up. Nicole shoved the pictures and the note back onto the shelf. There were many things Borley was not telling her. He did not seem like a professor at all, but more like a professional student found at any college. Perhaps he had landed a summer job that included an office and he was acting out a fantasy. There was his psychological study, which seemed pointless, almost amateurish. There was his toolshed, interesting at first but suddenly sinister in light of the note left by this Karen. There were his pained expressions in response to her innocent statements. But most of all there were the locked doors.

Nicole rolled the chair over to the file cabinets. Each drawer was labeled with a year: 1958, 1928, 1898, 1868. None was locked. She opened the drawer for 1958 and found it crammed with files. She ran her thumb over the names printed on the tabs. Borley's filing system obviously was not alphabetical. Sarah Grover followed Constance Young. Penelope O'Shea was between Margaret Seagle and Mary Ann Fitzgerald. The thickest file had no name on the tab, just the initials V. K. Nicole pried it from the drawer and spread it open on the desk.

Most of the file was white loose-leaf paper written on both sides in ink. The sheets were stiff and the pen strokes were blurry with age. It seemed to be a journal. The first entry was dated 10/20/58:

> *I met her on Cascadilla Bridge. It was June 17, and I had just come out of Triangle Bookstore. It was a sunny day and I wanted to drop off in the dorm room the textbook I had just bought.*
>
> *I never saw her. Sometimes I think she materialized out of thin air. I bumped into her so hard that my book almost fell into the gorge. She was carrying a sheaf of papers (I would later learn they were prints). They scattered on the pavement.*

Nicole flipped ahead. After several pages the name Valerie Kennedy appeared. Entries followed entries, detailing dates, conversations, thoughts. Pages were filled with the letter V, but nowhere was there a clue to the writer's identity. Then she came across the entry for 10/27/58:

> *We sat on the front porch swing, drinking beer and not saying much. The sun was behind the hills and the fields were turning blue. I was beginning to think that going there was a mistake. Then she spoke with purpose.*
> *"You know that I'm almost thirty, right?"*
> *I nodded.*
> *"And you're what, eighteen?"*
> *I gulped. Now it was out.*
> *"Does any of this bother you?"*
> *"No."*
> *"Good. Then I think we should be lovers."*
> *We went into the farmhouse and she led me upstairs to a narrow room with a daybed and dresser.*

*A large map of New York State hung above the bed.
I was so nervous I asked about the map. It must
have sounded stupid, but she whispered that the
farmer had put it there. She was so patient.*

*She lay on the bed. I joined her, trembling, my
hands and feet freezing. She knew. She kissed me
softly and said, "Borley," and everything was all
right.*

Nicole let the page fall. Things were beginning
to click. The toolshed was not an art gallery but a
replica of the room in which the teenage Borley
Share had first made love to an older woman
named Valerie Kennedy, who happened to be an
artist. Nicole skimmed forward. The writing lost
its coherence, as if Borley intended the words to
be meaningful only to himself, but she caught
vague references to "bad stuff," a Baby Valerie,
and sleepless August nights. She turned to the
last page, where he had carefully printed the
final entry:

*I no longer go to the police or to Missing Persons.
They are no help. Another man might despair, but
not I. I will find her, I will find her, I will find her. I
don't care how long it takes.*

Behind the journal was a poor photocopy of a
drawing of a woman's face. The woman looked
like the nurse in the photograph, and Nicole felt
the same vague nostalgia coming over her. In the
lower right-hand corner of the drawing were the
initials V. K. She quickly closed the file folder. A
small photo shot face down across the desk.

Printed on the back was: Valerie, circa 1956. She turned over the photo and her breath caught in her chest. Valerie Kennedy could have been her double.

Nicole shoved the file back into the cabinet. Borley could be back in five minutes or an hour. She was not going to gamble and she was not going to be anyone's doll. She called a local taxi office and arranged to have a cab meet her at the bottom of the cul de sac. Then she hurried into the bathroom and stuffed everything she could find into the overnight bag.

Nicole kept close to the thick shrubs that lined the front lawns of the neighboring houses. She was ready to dive for cover if Borley's car rounded the bend. The cab arrived just as she reached the corner. She sat low during the windy ride home, fending off the cabbie's attempts at conversation and wondering how someone as obviously disturbed as Borley Share had fooled her. He was certain to come looking for her. He knew her address, her telephone number, the places she hoped to work. He knew too goddam much about her. She had handled unhappy men in her past but never one obsessed with an image she happened to fulfill.

The cab stopped at the entrance to her apartment building. For once she wished she had a doorman. She gave the cabbie a large tip and ran into the building, chased by the strange sense that Borley was already nearby. The elevator was at the penthouse level. She jabbed at the button and kept an anxious eye on the front door as the elevator made its slow descent. Borley did not appear.

Nicole entered her apartment, dropped the overnight bag to the floor, and went into the kitchen to make a drink. As she ran water over the ice tray she had a feeling she was not alone. The idea was preposterous, but she decided to check. Then she would mix herself a stiff one, put her feet up, and plan how to handle Borley Share.

She peeked into the living room. No one was there. She looked behind the bathroom door and pushed back the shower curtain. Everything was in order. The bedroom closets were a mess and a pair of shoes she had forgotten she owned lay under the bed, but no one was hiding. She was beginning to feel stupid.

The last room was a second bedroom she used as a study. It had two tiny windows that faced east and, as dusk approached, always slipped into darkness before the rest of the apartment. She turned on the light. A tall man dressed completely in black sat on her desk with his legs crossed and his arms folded. Nicole's hand froze to the doorknob. A sly smile crossed the man's face and his eyes pulsed light.

"Hello, Nicole," he said.

She turned to run, but the door flew out of her hand and slammed shut. She found herself face to face with a woman in a nurse's uniform. She had seen the woman before—in the photos at Borley's house. She slapped at the woman's face, but the woman easily caught her wrist and squeezed. Nicole crumpled to the floor in pain. The woman lifted her to her feet like a child, smiled haughtily, then sent her spinning. Nicole landed on her back with her head almost under the desk.

"I told you to be gentle," the man said. He jumped off the desk, his boots landing heavily on either side of Nicole's head.

Nicole tried to scramble to her feet. The man's eyes brightened. An invisible weight fell on her stomach. Slowly, the man knelt. Nicole's legs kicked wildly, her arms beat the floor, her head shook, but she could not move the weight.

"She is the last one," the man said a million miles away. He touched Nicole's neck. The weight swallowed her and the room went dark.

Chapter Thirty-two

———◆———

IT TOOK CHARLIE twenty minutes to trace the Starion's problem to a defective relay switch and another forty minutes to replace the part. He limped around to the driver's side and reached in to turn the ignition. The engine exploded to life, then settled down to a steady hum.

"Sounds good to me," Borley said after a minute.

Charlie nodded, preoccupied.

"Seems like it's fixed," Borley said after another minute.

"Maybe." Charlie looked at his watch. "These things cycle for three minutes."

"Meaning what?"

"Meaning that we gotta wait another minute."

The minute passed with the engine still humming. Charlie slammed down the hood and declared the Starion cured.

"Cars are too goddam complicated these days," he said. He led Borley into the office and scribbled something on a bill that looked like "$62.00." "I lucked out finding that relay. Job coulda' taken all night."

"Glad it didn't," said Borley. He took sixty dollars out of his wallet, then dug into his pocket for two more.

"Forget it," said Charlie. "Cars are too damn expensive these days."

"Thanks," said Borley.

He eased the Starion out of the garage and quickly shot her into overdrive. Shadows covered the road, evening mist hung in the trees. In the distance, the traffic light at the crossroads turned red. Borley downshifted. The girl who sold the flowers was gone. Pink and yellow petals lay on the dirt where her truck had been.

Borley sensed trouble as soon as he turned into the cul de sac. Streetlights flickered in the twilight, and lamps burned in the neighbors' windows, but his house was completely dark. He skidded into the driveway, not bothering to let the engine cool or to take the shopping bag when he left the car.

The front door was not locked. He ran directly to the downstairs bathroom. Water dripped in the sink, and the rug was upset as if someone had run across it. He threw back the shower curtain. The sextant sat on the ledge, next to the bubble bath.

He staggered into the kitchen with the sextant in his hands. A blue flame licked in the darkness, and he became aware of a hissing sound. He turned on the overhead light. A steaming pot sat above the flame. He edged closer, watching himself here and in the kitchen of the farmhouse thirty years before. A drop of water jumped out and landed on the burner's grid. It hissed at him.

"No! Goddammit, no!"

He whacked the pot off the burner. It skittered across the counter, spraying boiling water on the walls and floor before clattering into the sink. He went into the study and punched Nicole's number on the phone, but did not wait for a connection. He slammed the receiver so hard that it cracked.

He blew through the kitchen, grabbing the gin bottle from the table without breaking stride. The cul de sac was quiet under the darkening sky. The stone steps were still warm from the afternoon sun. He sat down, placed the sextant beside him, and sidearmed the cap of the gin bottle into the grass. He took several pulls without tasting the gin, then stopped to feel it spread through him. This was his lot in life—to fall in love with a woman who vanished into August twilight. Then again, maybe he was not alive at all. Maybe the impact on Cascadilla Bridge had sent him arcing over the stone railing to the water rushing thinly over the shale bed hundreds of feet below, leaving him to drift in his own underworld.

Borley pointed the sextant at the deepening sky. Savage would have laughed at the idea of a modern day Tantalus, just as he had laughed at the theory of stimuli and chemicals and women who acted like sick cats. Savage. The big man had disappeared, maybe died doing a job—one hopeless romantic to another—and here he was sitting on the front stoop sucking gin.

Borley flung the gin bottle onto the lawn and dashed into the house. He found a crowbar in the cellar and a new clothesline in the kitchen pantry. He uncoiled the clothesline, placed it on a wooden cutting board, and, with a meat cleaver, hacked off several three-foot lengths. He secured the strips to his belt. As he searched through the study for his list of hospitals, the telephone rang. He lifted the cracked receiver. It was Moira.

"Borley, your woman is in the hospital."

"What is she doing?"

"I don't know. She walked past me and took the elevator upstairs."

"Where are you?"

"At the reception desk," said Moira.

"I'm on my way," said Borley. "Don't let her leave."

"I'll do my best."

Borley grunted thanks. He added a flashlight to his arsenal and hustled out to the Starion, picking the sextant from the front steps on the way.

He reached St. Catherine's quickly. Moira saw

him enter the lobby and she left the reception desk to meet him.

"Still here?" he said.

"I haven't seen her leave," said Moira.

"How many exits are there?"

"Many, but most of us use either this one or the ER. You remember where that is."

"Right," said Borley. "I can watch both of them from outside."

"What will you do?"

"Get some answers."

Borley took a position midway between two lights on the sidewalk running along the front of St. Catherine's. A patrol car rolled up to the emergency room entrance. People exited the lobby in small groups, children skipping, adults speaking solemnly. He checked his watch; visiting hours were over.

The police car left. The flow of people from the lobby tailed off. Borley paced a tight circle on the sidewalk, keeping in the shadows. He could see Moira behind the reception desk and a security guard leaning against the emergency room door.

The nurse came out of the lobby. She walked quickly, one arm pumping, the other supporting the heavy object he had noticed the other night in the pocket of her smock. She angled across the parking lot and entered a dark-colored van. Borley ran to the Starion. The van sat motionless for several minutes, then shook as its engine started.

Borley allowed her a good lead onto the street and followed her to Florence Hospital. He waited in the Starion until she went inside, then took the flashlight and the crowbar and zigzagged

through the parked cars to the van. The doors
were locked. He shined the flashlight's beam
through the passenger's window. There was no
partition behind the seats, so he could see clear to
the rear doors. The inner walls were bare metal.
The floor had a plain brown carpet littered with
crushed boxes from a men's clothing store. No
one was inside.

Borley returned to the Starion and resumed
his watch on the hospital doors. The nurse appeared within minutes. She started the van and
Borley was back on the road again. She led him
past the Shore Club and into Greenhaven, where
she made a sudden right turn onto an unlit private road. He waited until the taillights receded
into the darkness before he cut his headlights and
followed. The van returned to view, curving left
then right on the winding road. On either side
mansion windows flickered in the trees. The van
continued its descent. The smell of low-tide mud
thickened. Borley wondered how much road
could remain before they reached the water.

The van made a sharp right. Borley could see it
in profile now, ascending a slight incline. He followed through an opening in a low stone wall
onto a long driveway that forked at a screen of
pines. Up ahead, the van wheeled in front of a
large mansion whose towers and gables were
etched against a misty sky turned orange by the
distant lights of New York. Borley eased the Starion into the turn as the van stopped under a porte
cochere. The van's door opened and a white-
stockinged leg reached for the ground.

Borley felt her see him. The door slammed

shut and the van shot forward. Borley hit his headlights and accelerated. The van was on the far side of the circle, careening madly toward the driveway. Borley kept the Starion in a tight turn, the turbocharger whistling, the tires screaming. The van raced through the fork. The branches of the pines bobbed in the wash of air.

He was right on her tail. The van swerved in a desperate attempt to keep him at bay. The wall was approaching fast. He pulled off the driveway. The wheels spun on the grass, then caught, shooting the Starion past the van. He cut back to the right. Tires screeched. The van spun with him off the driveway and into a thicket just short of the wall.

Borley leaped out of the car with the crowbar in hand. The nurse frantically struggled to open the van's passenger-side door. Borley smashed the windshield, showering her with white pellets of glass. He punched a hole in the driver's window and reached in to pull the handle. She tore at his arm with her fingernails. He brought the crowbar down onto her elbow. She yelped and jumped back against the passenger door, her legs kicking. He caught one ankle, then the other, and yanked her to the ground. She tried to crawl away, but he grabbed the back of her smock and threw her up against the side of the van. He hooked the crowbar around her neck and snapped her head so her ear was at his teeth.

"Where is she?"

"Who?"

"Nicole Bourne."

"I don't know what you're talking about."

She was strong, but his anger made him stronger. He pulled the crowbar against her throat until she started to choke.

"Don't fuck with me," he said. Her body sagged. He felt around the front of her smock with his free hand and pulled out a silver canister. It was cold to the touch.

"What is this?"

"Medical equipment."

"Medical equipment my ass," said Borley. "I've been watching you in hospitals late at night, Dolly. I don't know what the hell it is you're doing, but it's not the practice of medicine."

He reached back to place the canister on the roof of the Starion. Dolingen, feeling the pressure lessen, tried to squirm away. He slammed her back into the side of the van and pulled on the crowbar.

"Let's go back to my original question," said Borley. "Where's Nicole?"

"I don't know."

"Is she in that mansion?"

Dolingen shook her head. The movement against the crowbar made her gag.

"Who lives there?"

"I don't know."

"You don't seem to know too much," said Borley. "Why the hell did you drive in here?"

"I was lost," said Dolingen. "I needed directions."

"Then why didn't you ask?"

"The mansion frightened me. Then I saw you. I thought you were a caretaker or a guard."

"I see," said Borley. He slowly let the crowbar fall away. Dolingen relaxed and rubbed her neck.

Borley jammed his knee into the base of her spine. Her hands dropped. He grabbed her wrists and lashed them together with a strip of clothesline from his belt.

"What do you think you are doing?"

"Making you more manageable." Borley tugged at her wrists. "Comfortable?"

"Hardly."

"Pity," said Borley, mimicking her affect. He removed the keys from the van's ignition, jingled them in front of her eyes, and dropped them into his pocket.

"Very well," said Dolingen. "Perhaps I can help you find her."

"Now you're being sensible," said Borley. He stuffed the canister into his shirt pocket. "I'll hold on to this as collateral."

"That hardly is necessary," said Dolingen.

Borley shoved her into the car and climbed behind the wheel. "Where is she?" he said.

"Take the road back to the highway and make a right. I will direct you from there."

Borley nodded. He backed the Starion out of the bushes and turned toward the mansion.

"I said to drive out of here."

Borley nodded again.

"Did you hear me?"

Panic edged into Dolingen's regal tone. She bucked in the seat. Borley shot out his fist and caught her in the corner of her mouth. She slumped against the door, babbling about the road, the highway, her directions. A thread of blood ran from her lips.

Borley drove slowly through the porte cochere,

noting the darkened windows and the huge wooden doors. He stopped the car in the shadows near a metal gate.

"Never did believe you, Dolly."

He went around to open the passenger door. Dolingen tumbled out, but he pushed her back.

"Why do you call me Dolly?"

He reclined the seat and rolled her onto her stomach. He tied her ankles, then bent her legs and tied her ankles to her wrists.

"Why do you call me Dolly?"

He tore a strip from the bottom of her whites and stuffed it into her mouth. He used the last piece of clothesline to keep it in place.

"You fooled me thirty years ago. You won't fool me this time."

Chapter Thirty-three

———◆———

BORLEY LEFT DOLINGEN in the car. He took the crowbar and the flashlight and used a key from Dolingen's chain to unlock the huge wooden doors of the mansion. He found himself in an octagonal foyer lit by a chandelier that hung from the center of a high ceiling. Eight mouthless gargoyles stared down from each corner.

He walked across the foyer and shined the

flashlight into a room decorated like a nineteenth century parlor. Clear plastic covered the red velvet upholstery of the sofas, chairs, and ottomans. The mahogany tables and shelves lacked ashtrays, vases, books, statues—anything to make the room look lived in.

He entered a dining room with a long oak table and a cathedral ceiling. Several pieces of furniture were covered with sheets, as were ten of the twelve chairs surrounding the table. The two uncovered chairs were opposite each other near the head. Before each was a clean white plate.

He went into a wrought iron library. The ladder for the upper tier of stacks lay on the floor, its wheels broken. He did not check whether the pages in the books were cut.

While he was in the library he noticed the bulbs in the foyer chandelier start to flicker. He held his breath and kept very still. The mansion was quiet except for a dull sound that throbbed like a heartbeat. He could feel the vibration through the floor.

The foyer had a small elevator, but the gate was locked and the cables indicated the car was down below. Borley hastily went through each of the rooms again. None provided any access to the basement. He returned to the foyer and studied the walls with the flashlight. Between the parlor and the dining room he noticed a door set so perfectly it disappeared into the wall. He pushed with his fingers and pulled with his nails. The door did not budge. He tried to insert the crowbar, but the seam was too narrow.

Borley went outside. He still could sense the

heartbeat rhythm in his ears and in the ground. He looked through the car window. Dolingen had not slipped her bonds. Their eyes met. She sneered.

Borley backed away so she could not see the direction he was headed. He quietly scaled the metal gate that separated the driveway from the service road. He walked carefully, the flashlight off, the crowbar at the ready. The rhythmic vibration strengthened with every step.

The foundation was covered with shrubbery, and the basement windows were dark. At the rear of the mansion he noticed a bush with twisted branches. He poked through and found several pinholes of light shining in the darkened glass of a window. He placed his eye against the largest of the pinholes. Below, in a basement workshop, dozens of large silver-and-glass cylinders stood exactly upright in the precise rows along the walls. One by one, with each throb of the heartbeat, the cylinders rose to a horizontal position and floated toward a faint green light beyond the workshop door. Each cylinder contained a woman wearing a silver bodysuit. Gina floated out of the room. A few cylinders later, Kate followed, her hair no longer the artificial blond she had admitted that day in his office. Their arms were at their sides, their eyes closed, their expressions serene.

Borley ran up to the Starion and removed Dolingen's gag.

"The police will deal with you," she said.

"Nice try, Dolly. But you know as well as I that

this isn't a police matter, not this year, not thirty years ago, not a hundred twenty years ago."

"I haven't the slightest idea what you are talking about."

"I'll explain what I've figured out so far. You tell me if I'm right," said Borley. "You have been implanting zygotes in women, then taking the offspring away at thirty-year intervals."

"Preposterous."

"Of course it's preposterous, which is why it's worked for so long," said Borley. "The children have intimations of the truth—dreams, fantasies, vague impressions of being different—but they eventually forget. Meanwhile, you slip in and out of their lives as you see fit. You watch them grow, keep them safe, and help them make decisions that serve your goal. If one wants to move to California, you dissuade her. If another becomes involved in a relationship, you break it up. I don't imagine you use the same technique on each. Sometimes you're a friend, other times you're a stranger who happens to say the right word at the right time. They listen to you, and when the time comes to take them away, they are so alienated no one misses them."

Dolingen sneered.

"I found the pattern in the disappearances and I found one of your mistakes. A woman named Grover became pregnant during a hospital stay sixty years ago. She was an unmarried virgin and was in the habit of switching beds with her roommate. Her daughter disappeared thirty years later. It didn't make sense to me until I watched you at Florence Hospital the other night." Borley tapped the canister in his shirt pocket. "This is where you keep the zygotes, right?"

"You are a veritable genius," said Dolingen.

"Not quite. It's taken me thirty years to piece that much together, but I still don't have the complete answer."

"Maybe in another thirty years," said Dolingen.

Borley yanked her arms. She winced in pain, but did not make a sound.

"Why are they in those cylinders? How do the cylinders float? Where the hell are you taking them?"

"All right," said Dolingen. "You have seen enough. There no longer is any harm in telling you."

Borley released her arms. Dolingen arranged herself on the seat as best she could.

"Your assumptions are correct," she said. "We are from a system fifteen light years distant that lies on a direct line with the constellation you know as Perseus. We are human and we live very long lives by your standards. Our resources are not devoted to the raising of children, so we use other planets as incubators. You may have noticed a resemblance among some of the children. That is because many of them are sisters, conceived on our world hundreds of your years ago."

Borley saw faceless couples entering a silver building beneath a purple sky.

"Why no males?" he said.

"We seed the males elsewhere," said Dolingen. "Too many of the young men on this world die."

"And every thirty years the women are ferried back?"

"The children," said Dolingen. "They are only children by our standards. And you are correct. The round trip takes thirty years."

Borley threw open the car door.

"There is more," said Dolingen.

"That's enough for me," said Borley. He jumped out of the car with the crowbar in his hand.

"Who was it?" said Dolingen. "Who did this to you?"

Borley stopped.

"I know the type of man you are. You did not just chance upon us. You must have known one of them. Who was it?"

"Valerie Kennedy."

"Ah yes, the artist."

"Were you the woman who encouraged her to paint?" said Borley.

"As a means of keeping her occupied until her time had come."

"And her parents' car accident on the way to Virginia?"

"You mean the surrogates?" said Dolingen. She leered. "Unfortunate."

"Did she ever mention me?"

"Don't flatter yourself," said Dolingen. She affected a thoughtful look. "Although I do remember a young boy who called at the farmhouse the night we took her away. He just missed us. Might he have been you?"

Borley slapped her. Dolingen's head snapped sideways, but she kept her composure.

"You think that she loved you because you loved her," she said. "Impossible. They are all incapable of love, and because they are, no one cares about them."

"There are people who care," said Borley. "And Valerie did love me."

"Playacting. Pantomime." Dolingen laughed. "I doubt she even remembers you."

Borley lunged. His hands found her neck. His thumbs pressed into her throat. She struggled, but his thirty years of loneliness and frustration were too strong. He shook her in time to the heartbeat that throbbed in the ground beneath the Starion. Dolingen's eyes rolled back.

Suddenly the car was still. Borley loosened his grip. The heartbeat had stopped. Dolingen gasped for air.

"I'm not going to be late this time," he said.

He ran down the service road and looked through the window. All of the cylinders were gone. He smashed the glass with the crowbar and jumped through. He landed near the large table and noticed Savage's business cards spilling out of an old wallet. It was one more reason to put an end to this game.

Beyond the workshop door, a faint green light emanated from a perfect circle in the foundation's wall. It was the entrance to a tunnel that descended in a slight, constant grade. The walls were glassy and warm to the touch. Beneath the surface were contours of earth, rocks, and roots. Borley guessed he had run about a quarter of a mile when the striations in the walls changed to mud and broken seashells. He knew he was under the harbor floor. Finally he reached a curtain of green light that seared his eyes. He covered his face with one hand and groped forward.

The light fell away and he stood in a large chamber filled by a spaceship too perfect to be real. The disk was the same silver metal of the cylinders. The domed superstructure had a faint greenish tint. Two beams of green light shot away from the top. One flew over his shoulder and entered the tunnel. The other played on the ceiling of the chamber. A vertical slit in the side of the superstructure slowly began to close. Borley vaulted onto the disk. The surface was slippery, but he managed to dive through the entryway just before it sealed.

He landed at the intersection of two corridors, one curving along the circumference of the superstructure and another leading straight to its center. A metallic sound echoed from somewhere deep within the ship. He edged toward the center. The sound stopped. He paused at the entrance to the main cabin. The domed ceiling glowed milky white. In the center, several instrument panels stood in front of a command chair half covered by a retractable canopy. Alcoves and doorways to other areas alternated around the wall. The metallic sound started again, coming from beyond a doorway to his right. Borley moved slowly as the sound stopped then started again. He could see the doorway led into a storage area. Cylinders covered the walls. They lay horizontally, their glass sides pointing upwards, the women's faces visible in profile. A man wearing a black jumpsuit and silver boots lifted a cylinder to the last available space. Nicole was inside the cylinder.

Borley crept to the edge of the door. Garno secured Nicole to the wall and loudly attached metal tubes to each end of her cylinder. When he stepped away, Borley struck with the crowbar. The impact shattered Garno's left arm and crashed into his ribcage. Garno slumped against the wall. Borley pounded him in the stomach. Garno doubled over, his breath rushing out of his mouth. Borley raised the crowbar high, aiming at the back of Garno's neck.

Garno lifted his head, his eyes ablaze. Borley brought the crowbar down, but his arms stopped. The crowbar ripped itself out of his hands and flew back into the cabin.

Borley grabbed for Garno's neck, but his hands would not close. He punched at Garno's face, but his fists bounced away from the mark. Garno slowly raised his right arm and pointed his finger at Borley. His eyes exploded like shooting stars. Borley felt the force of a battering ram strike his chest. He rose off the floor and flew backward, landing against the chair in the center of the cabin. Garno lowered his arm and staggered forward.

The force evaporated. Borley struggled to his feet. Garno stopped walking, a faint smile on his face, and began to take aim. Borley rushed him. He chopped down on Garno's arm and buried his head in Garno's chest. As they tumbled to the floor, Borley punched wildly. Garno threw him off. Borley jumped back. Garno spun away and rose to his feet. Borley tackled him.

They rolled into the storage area and crashed against the wall. The impact dislodged the cylinder containing Nicole. It fell on Garno's chest, pinning him to the floor.

Borley pushed himself to his knees, then to his feet. Garno struggled with the cylinder, but his left arm was useless and his right bore the full weight of the cylinder. Only his head was exposed.

Borley moved over him. Suddenly Garno's eyes brightened and the fingers of his right hand came alive. Before Borley could react the force hit him.

This time it focused on his stomach. It lifted him off the floor until he floated over Garno's head. Garno shook his finger; Borley spun like a whirlybird. He turned faster and faster, his hands and feet flailing. Then Garno flicked his finger. Borley flew off into the cabin, crashed against the far wall, and sagged to the floor.

Garno dislodged the cylinder and stood. Borley dizzily moved along the floor on his hands, his back flat against the wall. With his addled vision, he could make out the crowbar lying several feet away. Garno shuffled across the cabin. His left arm dangled. His right arm pulsated, its muscles growing larger. He reached the control panels in front of the command chair and pressed a button. There was a sound of rushing air, as if the entryway of the ship had opened.

Borley's hand touched the crowbar. He knew the command chair obstructed Garno's view. He grasped the crowbar firmly and slid it behind his back.

Garno moved around the chair. He stood over Borley, his boots firmly planted to discourage any attempt of escape. Borley adjusted his grip.

"You have no right to be here," said Garno.

"How ironic," said Borley. He flung the crowbar over his shoulder but it never left his hand. Instead, it slammed back against the wall.

Garno laughed. He slowly raised his arm. The crowbar moved up the wall, grinding Borley's knuckles and pulling him completely off the floor. The smile left Garno's face. His eyes narrowed into bright slits. His right arm swelled to twice its normal size, shredding the sleeve of his jumpsuit.

Borley knew that little time remained. He used his free hand and managed to dislodge Dolingen's canister from his shirt pocket. He held it up until he saw recognition in Garno's face. Then he let it drop. The canister rolled across the cabin floor. As Garno's eyes followed it, his arm moved enough to release the crowbar and Borley from the wall.

Borley landed on his feet and tomahawked the crowbar. It struck Garno on the side of the jaw. He reeled, his right arm flying up. A hole exploded in the ceiling, showering him with debris. Garno lay on his back, blood oozing from his mouth. His arm twitched as it deflated. He raised his head and tried to focus his eyes. Borley did not give him a chance. He kicked Garno across the temple and stamped on his throat until his eyes went dark.

Borley ran to the storage area. He felt along the seam of the fallen cylinder until he found the latch that released the glass lid. He felt Nicole's neck. She was warm, her pulse weak.

Chapter Thirty-four

———◆———

BORLEY PUSHED DOLINGEN through the entryway of the spaceship. She sprawled into the cabin. He grabbed her hair and dragged her to the storage area, where Nicole still lay unconscious in the open cylinder.

"Wake her up," he said.

"Impossible."

"You put her to sleep. You can wake her up."

"Even if that were so, I still choose not to."

"You are in no position to argue."

"To a rational being I could," said Dolingen. "What would be the purpose of waking her up? She does not belong here. Even if she wanted to stay with you, she would outlive you by hundreds of years, as Valerie would have. The only place for her is home."

"Home." Borley laughed. "I don't know who these women are, but I know what I went through the last time you took a bunch of women home. Forget your rational arguments about how their natures are not suited to living here. Valerie seemed to be living all right. Nicole, too. Until you meddled."

"It is not meddling," said Dolingen. "They do not belong here."

"And a lot of people here think these women belong with them. There's no need to debate who is right. I'm prejudiced and I'm calling the shots. Release them."

Dolingen did not move. Borley went into the cabin and began hacking at the control panels with the crowbar. Dolingen rushed to stop him, then noticed Garno on the floor beyond the command chair. She knelt over the body. By the time she stood, the panels were twisted metal stumps.

"You have killed Garno and you have immobilized our ship," said Dolingen. "But you cannot force me to release the children."

"Maybe, but I would say this to a rational being. This ship won't be missed for some time, and it will be even longer before anyone comes looking. Meanwhile, the government and its scientists would consider it buried treasure. You and the children would be tested, probed, and confined for the rest of your long lives."

Dolingen looked at the body and then at the control panels.

"Revive the women, return them to their lives, and leave them alone," said Borley. "Do that, and I won't reveal you."

"What about Garno?" said Dolingen. "Am I to ignore what you did to him?"

"He's a payback for Savage, the investigator."

Dolingen's lip curled into a sneer, but her eyes told Borley she was weighing the choices. She walked slowly to the storage area and removed an oddly shaped gun from a drawer in the wall. She placed its wide barrel against Nicole's left shoulder and squeezed the trigger. A blast of gas rushed into Nicole, leaving a wide circle of red on her skin. Nicole's whole body shook, then stopped. The red circle faded. Her pulse became visible in her neck.

Chapter Thirty-five

BORLEY AWOKE TO the smell of fresh coffee in the air. The smell transported him back to the summer he spent with Valerie, but he quickly realized that he was not in the farmhouse. He was home, and he was living with Nicole.

He found her sitting at the kitchen table, her eyes intent on a portable makeup mirror. A thick file folder leaned against the leg of her chair, and a coffee mug steamed at her elbow.

"You're up early," he said.

"Deposition this morning." Nicole made a precise stroke with eyeliner. "I wanted to review the file one more time."

Borley leaned over the sink and looked out the

window. An overnight storm had blown the last of the leaves from the maple tree. They speckled the newly planted evergreen shrubs that lined the backyard.

"Have you heard the weather report?"

"Clearing skies, temperatures in the forties, much colder later in the week. Why do you ask?"

"No reason." Borley poured himself a mouthful of coffee and quickly downed it. He started toward the bathroom, but Nicole hooked a long finger under the band of his shorts.

"What about the deposition?"

"A snap." Nicole wriggled her shoulders and let the bathrobe fall to her waist. "And it doesn't start until ten."

Borley watched from the bedroom window as Nicole's BMW sped to the bottom of the cul de sac and turned in the direction of the train station. It was seven-thirty, which left him little time to make his eight o'clock lecture. He dressed without taking a shower and went down to the basement. In one corner were stacks of food tins and cases of bottled water. He filled a cardboard box with a half dozen tins and two water bottles, then carried the box into the backyard. He made a slow circuit around the shed. The walls and roof looked undisturbed; the double padlocks on the door were secure. At the base of the side wall was a smaller door made of cast iron and hidden by two stubby evergreens. He unlatched the door and shoved the box inside.

Borley gave a lecture to his introductory psychology class and conducted a seminar in child development. In semesters past, he would seed his classes with oblique references to the disappearances in the hope of eliciting responses from his female students. This semester, he made no mention. His theoretical syndrome no longer was a syndrome and the women he had saved would be safer if the answer remained with him.

At lunchtime Kate Lyons was waiting for him in his office. She wore a conservatively cut business suit and had her black hair wound into a bun.

"How was Friday night?" Borley said after he started the tape recorder.

"You mean the dinner?" she said. "Fine. The twins' husbands are both very nice and they got along well with Marty."

"What about you and the twins?"

"Hard to say," said Kate. She grimaced momentarily, then relaxed. "They were surprised by the invitation and shocked to see me without my blond hair. They were cool at first. I guess they thought I had an ulterior motive, like maybe I landed a big-time modeling job and wanted to gloat. But I told them that I was working as a receptionist and that Marty's job had taken a turn for the better after the Houston convention. I told them we had our problems just like anyone else, but we were working on them."

"Sounds as if the dinner was a success."

"I'd give it a mixed review," said Katie. "We were polite, but there are years of bad feelings under the surface."

"How do you like your job?"

"I enjoy talking to people on the telephone and my secretarial skills are improving.".

"And your dream of stardom?" said Borley.

"Still there," said Kate. "But I've been keeping it in perspective, like you told me. Marty and I have a budget, so we don't argue about money. I save something out of every paycheck. When I have enough I'll invest in modeling lessons and a portfolio."

"Be patient," said Borley. "Your time will come."

"I hope you are right, Professor."

"Have I been wrong yet?"

Kate shook her head. Borley stopped the tape recorder and removed an index card from his desk drawer.

"The personal interview phase of the study is over," he said. "I'm writing a day and time on this card. Call me every fourth week."

Kate looked at the card, then inserted it into her wallet.

"You've done a lot for me, Professor Share," she said. "You've saved my marriage and made me believe that I can be happy. You should counsel people full-time."

"Maybe I will," said Borley.

Gina Lo Biasi called at precisely one o'clock. She was in buoyant spirits. Her attorney had won a major battle in the divorce proceeding against Ralph and it now looked as if she would receive a property settlement of two hundred fifty thousand dollars, plus the house. But her financial future was not the only reason for her mood.

"I met a man," she said. "Actually, my friend

Alice introduced me to him at one of those Wednesday night Shore Club dances. We hit it off very well. I've been completely honest with him. He knows all about my sterility and what it did to my marriage. And guess what? He says he doesn't care. He's even in favor of adoption."

"That's very nice," said Borley. If he had been functioning as a therapist, he would have told her to be wary of words uttered in the context of the singles' scene. But he was pleased with Gina's progress and said nothing to disturb her mood.

"How old is he?"

"My age," said Gina. "And he's a widower. Isn't that tragic, to be widowed at such a young age? So many people have problems, not only me."

"Keep me posted," he said.

The phone rang again immediately. A woman named Betty Simpson said she had received Borley's direct mail solicitation and wanted to become a part of his long-term psychological study. Borley pulled his master list from his desk drawer and made a check mark next to her name. All of the women had now answered.

Chapter Thirty-six

———◆———

NICOLE CALLED BORLEY late in the afternoon to say that the deposition had run long and she planned to work through dinner. Borley immediately left his office.

At home he went directly to the basement. A portable kerosene burner in a plain cardboard box lay on the workbench. It was designed as an inexpensive space-heater, but Borley had a slightly different use in mind. With a long wire, he connected a specially adapted thermostat to the burner's pilot. Then he constructed a heat duct out of a piece of sheet metal and a length of flexible metal hose. He attached the duct to the burner and tested the thermostat. It worked perfectly.

Borley carried the burner and his toolbox to the shed. The sun had long since set, so he worked by flashlight. He cut a six-inch circle in the wood near the base of the shed's rear wall. Then he carefully continued the circle through the layer of soundproof insulation he had installed in August. The pungent odor of toilet disinfectant reached his nose. The light of an electric lantern glowed weakly. Dolingen was visible within. She wore clothes from a Salvation Army store and sat Indian style on the sleeping bag.

"What are you doing?" she said.

"Installing a heater. It will be winter soon. You remember winter, I'm sure."

"Vividly," said Dolingen. "Does this mean I will sit here forever?"

"You will sit here until I contact the proper authorities."

"Authorities." Dolingen laughed. "You have been threatening me with the authorities for months. Do you take me for a fool, Share? You never will turn me over to the authorities. You will keep me here because you are too confused and too frightened to do anything else."

Borley dropped the thermostat into the hole and played out the wire until it reached the floor.

"You consider yourself vindicated," said Dolingen. "You consider yourself a hero. You are nothing but a fool. You don't know what you have done."

Borley fit the end of the duct into the hole and sealed the seam with putty. Dolingen's words became muffled, then finally trailed off into silence.

"I suppose this means that she will be our guest through the winter." Nicole leaned against the trunk of the maple. Her face, hands, and stockings caught the moonlight.

"Maybe."

"Maybe? I would say it looks damn likely."

"Let's not argue here," said Borley. He gathered his tools and led Nicole into the basement.

"This place looks like a bomb shelter," said Nicole. She pointed at the food tins and water bottles. "You've turned the backyard into a jungle with those evergreens. We can't invite people over. We can't go away for a weekend. And now you've winterized the shed. We're just as much prisoners as she is."

"It's necessary."

"Borley, I honestly don't see the harm in releasing her."

"I can't trust her."

"What is there to trust?" said Nicole. "You told me that she released us because she had no choice. She's just one woman."

"I still don't know enough about their activities," said Borley.

"Who cares about their activities? She released us—released me. Isn't that enough?"

"It's exactly why I'm so suspicious. She was too willing to cooperate."

Nicole hoisted herself onto the workbench and crossed her arms and legs.

"Then I think it's time you told me your intentions," she said.

"It seems to me," said Borley, "that Dolingen succeeded for so many generations because of the intense psychological pressure she exerted on the children. Most of them lived aimless, solitary lives, and the few who had relationships had bad ones. So when groups of women began to disappear at thirty year intervals, no one recognized the pattern because no one cared to look."

"Until you came along."

"Right. I confounded Dolingen's odds."

"That still doesn't explain why you won't release her."

"Most of these women are just as neurotic as they were in August. But with time and with professional help, they will be able to lead normal lives. If I released Dolingen now, there is no telling how much emotional havoc she might cause."

"Borley, your problem is you think too much."

"If I didn't, you wouldn't be here right now."

"Fair enough," said Nicole. "But why should you concern yourself with so many people?"

"I kept them here; I owe them that much."

"What about me? You kept me here, too."

"You are different from them, Nicole. I say that not because I love you but because it is true. You had the luxury of your relationship with Hugh. He helped you create a person that is strong enough to resist Dolingen. You don't need my protection. You can handle her quite easily. But right now only a few of the others have managed to strengthen themselves. When they all are ready for the truth, I'll release Dolingen. I need a little more time."

"All right," said Nicole. "A little more time."

Nicole sat with her back against the headboard. She could tell by the faint glow in the hallway that Borley was in the room he used as an office. She could hear the rumble of file cabinet drawers and the thin voices of women speaking over a tape recorder. He was working, tending to his flock, preparing them for the day when they would learn they were not of this world.

The full moon rode high in the sky, its light reflecting off the polished wood floor and illuminating the canvas on the far wall. She stared at the faceless couples, the silver towers, the three crescents in the inky sky and wondered whether Valerie's vision was fact or fancy. Without Borley's intervention, she would have been hurtling through space to that world, her memories of life here obliterated by artificial amnesia. She was grateful Borley had saved her, and even more grateful he had told her the truth about her nature, not kept her locked in ignorance as he had the others.

Nicole turned over at the sound of Borley's footsteps on the stairs. He undressed in the dark and slipped gently into bed. Nicole waited until he fell asleep. Then she quietly left the room, taking her bathrobe with her.

She went into the backyard and stared first at the moon and then at the shed. The burner suddenly choked off. The metal duct made clicking sounds in the cool night air.

"So, Nicole, you have come to visit me." Dolingen's voice echoed in the duct.

"How did you know I was here? The walls are soundproof."

"I can sense you," said Dolingen. "I can sense that you are troubled."

"I'm not troubled."

"Then why have you come to see me?"

"I'm not here to see you. I wanted to take a walk."

"Midnight walks never were your habit, Nicole, unless something troubled you. Is it Borley?"

"No."

"Ah, it is Borley." Dolingen laughed. "You finally have decided that you do not love him."

"That's not true."

"The way you decided that you did not love Hugh Michael Elliott, after you pumped him for his knowledge and his power, traded on his good graces to enter social circles you never could have known. And then, when he became too old, you forgot about him. Forgot about him because he reminded you of your own weakness."

"I loved Hugh," said Nicole.

"Oh, I know. We watched you make the arrangements, watched you at the wake, watched you at the funeral. The dutiful—daughter, was it? Lover? You lost me, Nicole. You always lost me. And now you say you love Borley. Won't you ever recognize that you are simply devoted to your own ego?"

"Shut up, you bitch," said Nicole. She ran into the house, chased by Dolingen's laughter. Borley stirred as she climbed into bed.

"Is anything wrong?" he said sleepily.

"No," said Nicole. "Nothing."

Chapter Thirty-seven

————◆————

THE NEXT AFTERNOON Borley noticed a man and a woman in the corridor of a shopping mall. Had he seen either of them separately he would have passed without giving a second look; together, they piqued his interest. The man had thick glasses and thin white hair. He was bent over a metal walker that his arthritis-ravaged hands barely could lift off the floor. The woman, who was much taller, held his elbow and offered encouragement as she guided him through the crowd. She wore a long coat that had been in style during Borley's youth. A veiled pillbox hat and round sunglasses covered her face, but a shock of rich, brown hair disappeared beneath her upturned collar. She struck Borley as a young woman trying to dress like an old woman.

Borley followed them into the parking garage. The woman folded the walker, then helped the man into a dark Lincoln Continental with a "handicapped" symbol on its license plate.

Borley telephoned the local state police barracks. The sergeant on duty was the father of one of his more promising psychology students. Borley asked for a computer check on the Lincoln. The sergeant told him to come right over.

A complete Department of Motor Vehicles computer printout was waiting at the desk. The registered owner was a William Van Riper. His license, which carried restrictions for corrective lenses and a hearing aid, had expired the previous year. He was seventy-seven years old. The only other licensed driver at the address was a Madeline Van Riper. She too was seventy-seven years old. Her license carried no restrictions.

Borley felt the same giddy excitement he had felt when he discovered the newspaper account of Mary Ann Fitzgerald's disappearance. He called Nicole at the office.

"I'm onto something important," he said. "Does the name Madeline Van Riper mean anything to you?"

"No."

"I saw her at the mall in the company of a feeble old man who happens to be her husband."

"Husbands often are feeble," said Nicole.

"Her driver's license lists her age as seventy-seven, the same age as Mr. Van Riper. But she looks much younger. I have a hunch she may be one of you."

"So, naturally you will offer your services to her as well."

"No," said Borley. He paused to let her sarcasm fade. "But she may be able to help me. I'm off to see her now. I don't know when I'll be home."

"Don't worry, I'm working late tonight," said Nicole. "Very late."

Borley reached the Van Riper home well after dark. The Lincoln was parked in the driveway, and several first-floor windows were lit. He moved cautiously through the shadows until he reached the edge of the backyard patio. Glass doors separated the patio from the dining room, and through open curtains Borley could see the Van Ripers seated at the table. William Van Riper supported himself with his elbows. His useless hands hovered near his ears while Madeline Van Riper fed him with a spoon. Without her hat and sunglasses, she looked like a woman of forty.

Madeline wiped William's mouth with a napkin, then helped him out of the room. Moments later, an upstairs window lit; half an hour later, it darkened. Madeline appeared in the dining room. She had changed into a floor-length purple gown with long conical sleeves. She dimmed the dining room chandelier to a glimmer and slid open the door.

Soft music reached Borley's ears. Madeline stepped onto the patio. She lifted her eyes to the stars and slowly raised her hands until they extended over her head. She held the pose for several minutes. When she lowered her arms Borley moved out from the shadows.

"Madeline Van Riper," he said.

She reacted with neither alarm nor panic. She simply turned in his direction and stared deeply into his eyes.

"Step into the light."

Borley moved close to the glass doors. He felt her eyes sweep him from head to toe.

"You are not a burglar," she said. "What do you want?"

"I need to talk to you about something very important."

"Talk," she said.

"Your driver's license lists your age as seventy-seven. You're no more seventy-seven than I am."

"I take care of myself," said Madeline.

Borley did not notice her move, but suddenly she was inside the dining room.

"You're one hundred seventy-seven, maybe."

"If this is a joke, I'm calling the police." She started to close the door.

"Wait," said Borley. "Garno is dead, the ship is disabled, and I am holding Dolingen as a prisoner."

Madeline stiffened.

"I think we had better talk," she said.

Borley stepped into the dining room. Madeline turned off the music, raised the lights, and joined him at the table. She had washed all traces of makeup from her face. Her skin was smooth, her features vaguely reminiscent of Nicole's.

"My husband is a light sleeper and needs his rest," she said. "Keep your voice low."

Borley told her the entire story from the day he met Valerie to the events of the past summer. Madeline listened silently, her eyes sometimes widening in amazement or focusing in recognition.

"I can't say that I am shocked," she finally said. "I told Dolingen years ago someone would eventually discover them. She refused to believe there was any danger. She has complete confidence in her abilities and she holds the intelligence of the inhabitants in low regard."

"You speak as if you aren't one of them," said Borley.

"I was born before the Civil War and met a man with a taste for rebellion. We never quite fell in love, but his attitudes influenced me. When my time for retrieval came, I resisted. Garno could not wait and the ship left without me. For thirty years, Dolingen and I struggled physically, mentally, and psychically. When she realized she could never retrieve me, she offered a truce. I could remain here unmolested as long as I did not interfere with her.

"My life has been happy. I have had three good husbands. They have loved me and I have honored them. When William dies, I will disappear and re-emerge elsewhere."

"I hope the others can follow your example in time," said Borley.

"I doubt they will have the chance," said Madeline. "You may have killed Garno and disabled the ship, but you have not destroyed their work. Dolingen lied about help being thirty years away. There is a transfer base barely one light year distant."

Borley stared at the table. His mind raced with the implications of this new revelation.

"That *is* the simple solution, isn't it, Professor Share?"

"What is?"

"You are thinking of killing her."

"I'm weighing one hundred fifty lives against one."

"One hundred fifty ignorant lives, I should remind you, minus your Nicole. But you have already appointed yourself their guardian, a task I do not envy. So tell me how the death of Dolingen would save the rest."

"If there is no Dolingen when help arrives—I assume you believe help will arrive."

Madeline nodded. Borley continued:

"Then there wouldn't be anyone here who knows their whereabouts."

"A nice idea," said Madeline. "But whoever arrives to retrieve the children will find them, with or without the help of Dolingen. No, you will need her. Your best course would be to strike a deal using her as your pawn. Perhaps you can save your Nicole from retrieval."

A voice called weakly from upstairs. Madeline checked her watch and frowned.

"Professor Share," she said, "I cannot say that you brought me very good tidings tonight. You have muddled into something quite large and you have jeopardized my well-being as well as your own. I wish you luck, but I cannot foresee a pleasant result."

Nicole did not work as late as she had told Borley. In fact, after his phone call she did not work at all. She sat in her office and analyzed how Borley's discovery of Madeline Van Riper would affect her. Borley wanted the woman to help him. Help him with what? The only logical answer was to help him with his crusade to strengthen the psyches of the other women. Certainly, under Borley's theory, the women would then be able to resist Dolingen's psychological pressure. But there would be an unintended consequence: the women would become her equals.

As Borley sat in the Van Riper house, Nicole stood at the door to the shed. One hand held a bundle of winter clothes, the other held the forbidden keys. She unlocked the padlocks and threw open the door. Dolingen rose slowly from the sleeping bag. She had lost weight since August. Her skin was sallow and her hair was tangled.

"You are free to go," said Nicole. "But only on condition that you leave me and Borley undisturbed."

"After what he has done to me, after what he has done to Garno?"

Nicole pushed her to the floor.

"You and Garno mean nothing to me. Leave me and Borley alone. The others are yours."

Dolingen grinned beneath her curtain of hair. She had made a similar deal out of expedience once before and she saw no harm in doing the same now.

"Borley will not approve," she said.

"I can handle Borley," said Nicole. She dropped the clothes at Dolingen's feet and left the shed.

Epilogue

———◆———

SHE MOVED SHAKILY through the brush, the tattered parka wrapped tightly around her shoulders, her feet slipping into holes hidden by dead leaves. She paused at the top of the service road. Early morning sunlight played through the mist. A curtain billowed in a broken window. Graffiti scarred the mansion walls, calling her a witch, a demon, a woman who slept with dogs.

She lowered herself through the window Borley had smashed. The basement floor was covered with muddy footprints and swirls of damp rubbish. All traces of their activities were gone. The tunnel entrance was sealed with stone. She climbed out the window and continued down to the water.

The tide was out. She walked among the remains of a seawall until she found the stone she knew Garno had marked. She shouldered it aside. Dank air billowed past her face.

The chamber was dark. The ship was crusted with a layer of dried mud. She found the entryway to the dome and entered the code into the lock. Nothing happened. She entered a second code and felt the faint hum of the auxiliary power supply coming to life. The ship trembled as the entry slit opened.

She scrambled over heaps of empty cylinders until she reached the cabin. Garno, encased in a cylinder, rested on his command chair. The remains of the controls gleamed as energy reached the cabin lights.

She made her way to the forward hold and the panel she had noticed while reviving the children. She pulled the panel from the wall. Behind it, the lights of the emergency transmitter blinked in steady cadence.

She encoded a message to repeat itself ad infinitum. Then she sat down to wait.

Reading—
For The
Fun Of It

Ask a teacher to define the most important skill for success and inevitably she will reply, "the ability to read."

But millions of young people never acquire that skill for the simple reason that they've never discovered the pleasures books bring.

That's why there's RIF—Reading is Fundamental. The nation's largest reading motivation program, RIF works with community groups to get youngsters into books and reading. RIF makes it possible for young people to have books that interest them, books they can choose and keep. And RIF involves young people in activities that make them want to read—**for the fun of it.**

The more children read, the more they learn, and the more they **want** to learn.

There are children in your community—maybe in your own home—who need RIF. For more information, write to:

RIF
Dept. BK-3
Box 23444
Washington, D.C.
20026

Founded in 1966, RIF is a national, nonprofit organization with local projects run by volunteers in every state of the union.

NEENA GATHERING

VALERIE NIEMAN COLANDER

It's the twenty-first century and America is no more. The U.S. has split into sections and destroyed itself with chemical warfare. A civilization based on technology, communications, mass transportation, factories, schools, culture, and medicine has ceased to exist. Forced to grow up quickly under such conditions, can Neena eke out a living while fighting off roving bands of survivors as well as the misguided attention of her uncle, Ted? Or will she choose to become the symbol of a reborn nation with the horribly scarred but loving Arden?

ISBN: 0-517-00643-X   Price: $2.95